Bound by Nature

Bound by Nature

Cooper Davis

SAMHAIN PUBLISHING

Samhain Publishing, Ltd.
577 Mulberry Street, Suite 1520
Macon, GA 31201
www.samhainpublishing.com

Bound by Nature
Copyright © 2011 by Cooper Davis
Print ISBN: 978-1-60928-000-0
Digital ISBN: 978-1-60504-964-9

Editing by Tera Kleinfelter
Cover by Amanda Kelsey

First Samhain Publishing, Ltd. electronic publication: March 2010
First Samhain Publishing, Ltd. print publication: January 2011

Dedication

To Lulu for loving Hayden and Josh almost as much as I do, and for being a true sister of the heart.

Prologue

The commuter plane skidded as it touched down on the icy Wyoming runway. Eyes closed, Hayden cringed, reminding himself that the landing was always bumpy whenever he came home. All told, this journey had taken eight hours, door to door. Eight excruciating and claustrophobic hours for a wolf born to roam freely. This final portion of the journey, however, always killed him worst of all. Folding his six-foot-four frame into the small puddle-jumper that flew from Salt Lake to Jackson was achingly uncomfortable, and for an Alpha wolf like him, confined spaces were nearly unbearable.

Still, there was no way he'd have spent the holiday back in his dorm room at Dartmouth, and not just because it was Christmastime. After months around "normal" humans, he'd become what his kind called pack-lonely and yearned for the companionship of other wolves.

Hayden had inherited his father's Alpha streak—and it was displayed visibly in his monumental size, although physical stature wasn't the only element that determined true Alpha status within any pack. Of even greater importance were keen intelligence, dominance and will—

all three of which Hayden knew he possessed in spades. When his father stepped aside, Hayden would assume leadership, but hopefully that time was a long way off. He was still young—not quite twenty-two years old—and had exams and his political science thesis on his mind. Actually utilizing such theoretical knowledge to guide his people was the farthest thing from his thoughts.

He was just glad to be back on his home turf, smelling the fresh snow and the distant, earthy scent of his pack's land. After the long weeks of cramming for finals, the thought of running free across their territory sent a jolt of power through Hayden's veins. He already felt more alive than he had in months and he hadn't even reached the exit door yet. As he stared out the plane window at the mountains, his inner wolf sang in reaction.

Slinging his laptop case over his shoulder, Hayden ducked through the plane's hatch, stepping onto the slick steps that temporarily adjoined the plane. As he began climbing down, a blast of frigid Wyoming air hit his face, fogging over his wireframes. He hesitated, fumbling to remove the glasses, but missed the last step, nearly tripping onto the tarmac. He might have been an Alpha, but his chronic eyesight problems still caused occasional klutzy moments when he was in human form.

"Smooth move, Garrett." Raspy, rumbling laughter followed the words. "I see college has polished away all those rough edges of yours."

Of all the damned luck. Hayden glanced around, squinting, but without his glasses, everything was a blur. Still, he didn't need twenty-twenty vision in order to recognize that throaty voice. It belonged to a volatile Alpha wolf, one he'd known and competed with since childhood. His neck prickled with a mixture of dread and arousal—familiar sensations whenever he encountered Joshua Peterson.

"Hey, Josh." Hayden kept his tone as unrevealing as possible, an almost Herculean task considering the way his heart was leaping out of his chest.

"Home from New Hampshire, huh?" the other Alpha asked nonchalantly.

"It's that time of year," Hayden answered blandly. He should've kept on walking, but he was frozen there, caught in Josh Peterson's high-beams like he'd always been—and for almost as long as he could remember.

"Busy time of year, that's what." Josh leaned casually against an empty baggage cart, and even in blurry outline, was clearly as cocky as ever. Strong forearms were folded over a thick chest in obvious defiance—defiance against a fellow Alpha wolf.

"So you work here now?" Hayden asked. Last he'd heard Josh had been employed at a ranch over in Idaho, commuting back and forth over the mountains.

"Wrangling baggage these days, not horses," Josh answered with a gruff laugh, moving toward him with a clipboard gripped in his right hand.

"Seems like a good gig," Hayden said with a glance around the tarmac. They'd always lived such different lives, with Josh clawing and scraping for every opportunity he'd ever won, whereas Hayden had been born to money and privilege.

"Decent enough, I guess." Josh shrugged, pointedly studying his clipboard for a moment.

Hayden wiped off his glasses, then seized the opportunity to steal a yearning peek at the guy. He could barely swallow a gasp at what he saw as he centered his wireframes over his eyes. Good God above, Josh had changed physically since Hayden had last seen him nine months ago. His stocky frame had become more muscular, with powerful arms that bulged and pulled beneath his parka as he moved. That already handsome face of his had become even more stunning, too, and a dark beard dusted his jaw and chin. He wore a ski cap pulled low over his brow, and soft, unruly curls spilled out from underneath the wool. With his dark hair longer than Hayden had ever seen it, Josh now sported a pirate-turned-ski-bum allure. But all of that, as breathtaking as it was, was the least interesting surprise.

It was all about the other wolf's eyes. They'd always been mesmerizing, truly lovely. But their piercing, luminous green-gold depths had intensified, new flecks of light blue and amber accentuating their rare beauty. Hayden confirmed that change when Josh glanced up from his clipboard, clicked his pen shut and swung his light-eyed gaze right on him. A thrill rang through the center of Hayden's chest as they stared at each other, saying nothing for several long heartbeats.

Hayden had already been struggling with a serious hard-on just from being next to the man, but Josh's single, arresting glance made his jeans tighten uncomfortably. His hardened cock pressed against his zipper, his balls tightened and his entire groin began to ache. Thank God he'd worn his parka. Without its coverage, everyone on the tarmac would have seen exactly how Josh Peterson affected him. And Josh would have seen too—no doubt lifting a challenging eyebrow when he noticed the damning, bulging evidence in the front of Hayden's pants.

Which would've only been the beginning. Under Josh's subtle inspection, Hayden's arousal would have twitched and leaped enthusiastically, the prominent tent in the center of his jeans swelling even more. And at this, well, Josh would have laughed softly, amused as always by Hayden's hopeless lack of control whenever they came in contact.

Not this time, Hayden thought with a soft growl, and yanked his parka securely over his hips, although it was obvious Josh had already pegged the situation perfectly. His vibrant eyes sparkled with amusement, and he nodded his head knowingly, the corners of his full lips turning up at the edges into a smug, self-satisfied smile.

Damn, damn, damn, Hayden cursed inwardly, he sniffed out my arousal.

Sometimes it sucked being a werewolf, especially in the presence of another one—one who did some kind of sneaky voodoo magic on your hormones just by plain fact of existence. A fellow Alpha who didn't—and never would—return the sentiment.

If Hayden didn't do something to seize control of this situation, he was going to crash and burn, big time.

13

Interestingly enough, however, it was Joshua who tried to get the conversation back on track.

"So, home for the holidays." Josh sang the partial refrain of the song. "That's cool. But they don't get snow back in New Hampshire?" The other Alpha laughed with surprising softness, and Hayden found himself wanting to say far too much.

"Missed home. The folks." He looked around, making sure no one was listening, and lowered his voice confessionally. "Really missed my people...all our people."

Hayden hoped Josh would catch his deeper meaning. How he longed to be around their own kind, rival packs or not. Those differences didn't mean crap when you needed the companionship of other wolves. Thank God he was almost done at Dartmouth and would be back here in Wyoming for good in less than six months.

Josh's smile became sympathetic. "Tough being alone I bet," he agreed. "None of our people out that way?"

"Our people" was a sort of Mafia code phrase for fellow werewolves, and had always made Hayden laugh. He usually half-expected some consigliore to show up and start quoting The Godfather.

"None of the peeps." Hayden shook his head.

"Maybe you want to step out while you're home?" Josh suggested in a friendly tone. "Get a beer, go hit the trails..."

Now, what the hell was this?

The two of them didn't run together, not as humans or wolves. They never had, except...there'd been one night after Hayden's freshman year of college when he'd gone out hunting alone. After months away, he was thrilled to be back in the valley, feeling the beating rays of the full moon on his wolf's back. The way the summer breeze blew over the land, rippling his fur, awakening his ancient instincts.

He'd stopped to lap a drink from the river when he scented another wolf nearby. Looking up, he discovered Josh Peterson in wolf form, standing on an outcropping. The other Alpha was positioned over the river, bathed in silver moonlight. He was much larger than Hayden ever would have imagined, yet possessed a surprisingly sleek and compact elegance. Dark fur covered his entire body except for two places—his chest, which was marked by a thick tuft of white, and then his ears, which were white as well. His beautiful, unearthly eyes shone in the night, gleaming like those of a glorious predator.

After a moment in the other wolf's thrall, Hayden came crashing to his senses, long enough to panic. Josh's presence meant Hayden had inadvertently veered onto the other pack's land, violating the treaty between their two clans. By all rights Josh could—and should—have challenged him for the transgression. Instead, Josh had tilted his wolf's head sideways, sniffing the air and studying Hayden intently. Then, he'd made a light yelping sound, a playful, inviting one, and they'd taken off together on a spectacular run. Josh had shown him places he'd never discovered before, special spots that were off limits to Hayden's own pack. The bond he'd felt, running and hunting with the other wolf, had transcended anything he'd ever experienced before...or since.

Josh's laughter brought him back to the moment. "Yep, still our same Hayden. Daydreaming like always."

Hayden scowled at him. "I'm not your Hayden."

Josh only rolled his eyes, unaffected by Hayden's barking tone. "Yeah, whatever." And then he smiled, a genuine, beautiful thing, and all of Hayden's natural defenses melted away. "So what about making a plan, dude?" Josh asked casually. "You up for a night out? It's been too long."

All right. Act like this is normal, no big thing. Hayden cleared his throat, pushing his glasses up his nose, then ran a hand through his short hair. "Yeah, sounds cool," he said, then shoved both hands in his jacket pockets in an effort to stop his anxious fidgeting. "Maybe get a couple of beers, sure."

"Moon's up on the twenty-ninth," Josh volunteered, eyes gleaming suddenly.

Hayden's chest tightened sharply. So Josh wasn't suggesting a casual drink, but something much more intimate: a run together at the moon's peak cycle, when their bodies and hormones—and transformative energy— would be bursting forth from their wolf forms.

Still, as thrilling as the prospect was, something didn't seem right. Maybe Josh's dad had put him up to this invitation, hoping Hayden might spill pack secrets, or slip up and reveal too much.

"Maybe," Hayden said with a noncommittal shrug.

"Call me."

Josh blinked back at him, clearly not understanding Hayden's sudden aloofness. "Should I call you?" he asked quietly, uncertainty flashing in those mystical, magnetic eyes of his.

Hayden shrugged again. "Sure, that's what I said. I'm up for a night out."

Another airline employee called to Josh, and he held a finger out to Hayden. "Hang on a sec, man. Be right back." He moved away, adjusting his headset, apparently receiving some direction. Hayden watched, feeling the familiar burn of desire in every part of his body.

Growing up in the Jackson area, and being the same age, had meant that Hayden and Josh were constantly crossing paths. Competing for positions on athletic teams, or top grades in class. Their secret rivalry, however, was far more intense: they were both Alphas being groomed to assume their fathers' leadership roles when the appropriate time arrived.

Hayden wasn't an idiot, either. It was pretty obvious that Josh had taken some heavy shit because he hadn't matched Hayden's own academic achievements. The politics between their two clans made him nuts. All of it was so ridiculously antiquated and competitive, especially if a wolf had even a slight Alpha strain in his blood.

Everything was a source for squabbling between their two packs. Land, resources, mates, animal rights. Almost any disagreement had the potential to set off months of fighting, which had made growing up in a small town, constantly around the sons of rival pack members, nasty business at times. Still, no one had ever gotten in Hayden's craw like the rugged, handsome Alpha who stood over at the airline desk right now.

Josh gave off a scent unlike any Hayden had ever known, one filled with intelligence, hidden wit, dominance...and a thousand other nuances Hayden simply refused to analyze. But as he always did whenever around Josh, Hayden reacted powerfully, instinctually...like the absolute wolf he was at heart. Well, absolutely gay wolf, was more like it.

Hayden had known he was queer since he was fifteen, had told his family as much at sixteen. Their pack knew it; the townsfolk knew it. Hell, Josh obviously knew it, same as all the rest of their acquaintances. On the other hand, Josh was as straight as any man ever got, Alpha or otherwise, so there was no point to all of Hayden's yearning. In fact, Hayden would have done anything to stamp out the unrequited attraction.

Hell, wasn't attending college thousands of miles away a respectable enough attempt?

Josh trotted back toward him. "Sorry about that," he called out with a wave of his clipboard. "Anyway...." His husky voice trailed off.

There wasn't anything more to say. The whole ridiculous conversation was an exercise in humiliation, at least as far as Hayden was concerned. He never should have gotten so excited about the idea of a night out with the guy. As it was, he was standing here on the cold tarmac, with a throbbing erection and balls that really might turn some shade of blue at any moment. Yeah, he'd name that color Bruised Ego Blue.

Hayden rocked back and forth on his feet, searching for something to say. "So, yeah, you're gonna call me," he finally blurted, all his previous hesitation taking off like one more plane taxiing down the runway.

Suddenly Josh's luminous eyes widened perceptively. And there it was again, his cocksure, knowing smile.

God, but Hayden wanted to haul off and plant his fist in the middle of that smug grin. Knock it right off the guy's gorgeous face. Yeah, Hayden knew he had to be absolutely reeking of lust, a strong scent that couldn't be missed by any fellow wolf. Things had gone this way between them on dozens of other occasions—with Hayden forever trying to hide his arousal and insane desires while Joshua left him hanging, amused to watch Hayden struggle.

Damn, but Hayden suddenly wished he'd never left New Hampshire.

"Better go," he said, attempting to force brightness into his tone. Only the words came out much sultrier than he'd intended.

Hell, even his voice was betraying him now, he thought, feeling his face flush, and not from windburn.

"Yeah, getting hot out here, isn't it, Hayden?" Josh smiled up at him, his bright-eyed gaze pure innocence.

You bastard. The heat crept from Hayden's face, all the way into his neck. Of course Josh didn't want to go out on a run or be drinking buddies. He'd been mocking him all along, having a little fun at the gay wolf's expense.

Mortified, Hayden muttered a lame goodbye and set off across the tarmac to the terminal, stepping gracefully around patches of ice and snow. Thanks to his very long legs, he was to the terminal in no time, but not before Joshua's damned husky voice and scent appeared right behind him.

"Hayden." Josh's hand came around him, pressing the door shut before he could open it. Hayden stared at Josh's forearm, braced only inches from his own shoulder, rippling with barely checked strength. Josh's parka sleeve rode up, revealing a muscular arm dusted with curling, dark hair. It was truly a man's arm, no longer that of a boy.

He didn't remember Josh being so physically mature in the past. Somewhere along the way, he'd grown from a pup into a strong, virile Alpha wolf, which only made him more dangerously alluring.

"Hayden," Josh repeated, his voice even softer. "Hayden...just look at me. Please."

He would not turn around. Josh had given him shit and tortured him for as long as he could remember, and even though it was all a bunch of Alpha male posturing, it still stung.

Josh's heavy hand came down on Hayden's shoulder. "You forgot your bag." His voice was strong and firm, and even—was it possible—apologetic. "You were supposed to pick it up out there, by the plane."

Hayden nodded, turning slightly, and Josh was right

up against him, clouds of condensation forming with each breath. He was huffing slightly from having sprinted to catch up with Hayden's much longer strides. As Josh offered him the bag, their hands brushed together, sending a shower of electricity through Hayden's entire body.

"Thank you, Joshua," Hayden said formally, and with a slight smile, opened the door. "I'll see you around soon, no doubt."

"How you getting out to your folks' house?" Josh called after him. He just wasn't going to let it go. For a solidly straight ladies' man, he certainly was persistent.

"Taxi," Hayden said simply, wanting to get away from the other guy with an almost fevered itch.

"Nah, nah, that won't do. Not for an old friend." Joshua shoved past him as Hayden wheeled his bag. "Lemme see if I can take an hour from work and give you a lift. Snow's starting up again, too, and supposed to get heavy real quick. Those taxi drivers aren't safe sometimes."

Then, Josh was off, chattering away on his headset, moving with the same fluid power Hayden had always admired in him. But why would Joshua Peterson care about giving him a ride home, or even call him an "old friend"? They'd been nothing more than acquaintances...except for one midnight run three years ago.

Hayden broke into a cold sweat. He couldn't do it, couldn't bear up for a thirty minute drive in the same car with Josh—not looking into those eyes, not feeling the heat radiating off his gorgeous, straight-guy body. His own body would naturally respond, releasing strong scents all its own—the arousal scent, the mating scent, the seduction one. God, probably a half dozen or more definable odors would be seeping out of his pores, betraying his not-very-secret attraction. Josh would probably smirk about it for years and years afterward. No way, wasn't going to happen.

Hayden started walking toward the curb and fast, ready to hail a cab, but then suddenly Josh was beside him again, reaching for his bag.

"Got it," Josh said and pointed to the main parking lot. "My truck's over here."

This was a bad, terrible idea. Because Josh knew. He'd always known how attracted Hayden was to him— and always left him twisting in the wind about it.

Right then, Joshua tilted his face toward the sky and started sniffing. The familiar, smug smile slowly returned to his face. "Thought I caught an unusual scent in the air," was all he said, walking again.

Hayden stood stock still where he was, releasing a spattering of curses under his breath. Josh glanced back at him, surprise in his light-colored eyes. "What?" he asked innocently. As if he hadn't just remarked on the arousal scent Hayden was throwing off like steam after a summer rain.

Hayden shook his head, clenching his fists against his thighs. "I'm not doing this," he said. It was high time he got firm with the object of his attraction.

Josh stopped and faced him, looked genuinely surprised. "Not doing what?" he asked, cocking his head sideways.

"I'm not going to ride in your damned truck, that's what." Hayden could feel the hair rising on the back of his neck, could sense his chest beginning to sprout slight fur. He was so worked up, he could hardly hold back his transformation. Not exactly a good idea, at least not here in public.

Josh seemed genuinely confused, and no wonder since Hayden had just gone Alpha on him over a polite offer of a drive home. Well, and Josh's smartass crack about catching Hayden's arousal scent on the air.

Lifting both hands up innocently, Josh's eyes widened. "Whoa, buddy. No problem. Ease down, okay?" He laughed as if embarrassed on Hayden's behalf, then pointed back to the curb. "Cab line's right over there."

Hayden couldn't get his reaction under control. nostrils flared, his lungs dragging at the rustic aroma radiating off the other man. "Thank you," he said, about to turn. But then Josh was directly in front of him, staring him down.

They pressed close, chest to chest, each heaving hot breaths at the other. For a moment Josh's eyes narrowed, the color turning much darker—with anger or...something else Hayden could've sworn he almost scented off the other Alpha?

Hayden wasn't going to back down. He'd come this

far, and standing up to his long-term nemesis felt invigorating. He had nothing to lose by simply being blunt and putting the truth out there, finally.

"I may never get the nerve to do this again, so I'm going to say it now," Hayden said. "You've always been amused by the strong scents I put off whenever you're around. Gotten off on how...how attracted I am to..."

He couldn't bring himself to finish, but it was more than obvious that Joshua caught his full meaning. He blinked in surprise, the lighter hues returning to his eyes, and Hayden would have sworn a slight flush hit his cheeks. "Hayden," the other wolf said quietly, staring at his boots, "I'm really sorry if you think—"

Hayden cut him off in a rush of sudden confidence. "Forget the lame apologies. I see it in your face every time. Subtle, mocking amusement about how I react to you. Well, you know what?" Hayden stepped closer, lowering his voice as he whispered the last into Josh's ear. "I'm a werewolf, Joshua. Maybe I can't help how I naturally react to your scent...and you. Maybe it's nothing more than nature kicking in."

Hayden sniffed Josh's face dramatically, lingering as he did so to drive his point home. His pants tightened in automatic reaction to Josh's heady scent, his cock filling with blood and heat all over again. He swallowed hard, keeping his mouth close to Josh's ear.

"I can't control my instincts, Josh, but I can choose whether I respect you or not. You think it's hysterical that I'm gay? Fine. I think it's hysterical that you're a small-town loser with no real future." Hayden took two steps back, holding both palms up. "I've always liked you. I used to respect you, but I'm done here. Done with you."

He spun, and put as much distance between himself and Joshua as he possibly could.

Josh scowled, watching Hayden stalk off to the cab line. He'd honestly been looking forward to catching up with the guy, excited when he'd spotted his distinctive, tall frame exiting the airplane. Josh had recognized him instantly; few men were so massive without appearing overbearing. But Hayden Garrett had always been surprisingly gentle for such a large man, with a body anyone would admire for its elegant power and controlled strength.

Josh rubbed his stubbly beard, trying to figure out how he'd managed to offend the other wolf. Hayden was so twitchy, always had been, but then again you didn't attend a school like Dartmouth and maintain a 4.0, majoring in...well, all kinds of shit, apparently. Josh had even heard Hayden was working to finish his honors thesis at the moment. Anyway, you weren't special like that without being a little...unusual. Sensitive. Whatever.

The thing was, Josh really had wanted to catch up with Garrett. Was curious what life was like off at college since he'd never get the same shot himself, especially not with an Ivy League school. Hayden had his entire future carved out for him, seemed to be shooting straight for the stars, whereas Josh only had the promise of one day serving as pack Alpha. He wasn't exactly going anywhere outside their small, secretive world.

They trotted two different trails in life, which might've made another wolf jealous, but for Josh, he was insatiably curious about Hayden's world. It wasn't like the two of them had ever been friends, not precisely, although Josh had tried making overtures on numerous occasions. But Hayden was just too defensive, and about most topics, including that long-standing crush he'd just brought up.

The main problem with Hayden was he was so damned intelligent, he tended to assume other guys were the same way. He didn't realize his unique mind was in a class all by itself—or that Josh had never been making fun of him or laughing. He just didn't have such complicated agendas. Yeah, he knew Hayden had a thing for him, and no, he wasn't gay himself. That was why he always smiled at Hayden, or "smirked" as the guy put it. Josh couldn't help it: the situation made him feel a little shy and uneasy. No other man had ever been into him, and certainly no one nearly as smart and powerful as Hayden Garrett.

Josh wished Hayden would just let that crap go because he seemed like a possible friend. Well, perhaps friendship wasn't quite the right word for it, but they'd always been on the brink of something significant. Something that never fully materialized because of the macho Alpha posturing that reared between them. They stayed on the verge of connecting, yet kept missing the mark.

Josh sighed heavily, walking back to the front of the airport, and was going to head inside when he spotted Hayden over in the cab line. Noticing his massive height and broad shoulders and short-cropped, dark hair...well the sight just ticked him off.

Damn it, the ridiculous bickering between their two clans had gone on long enough. Here was a solid, intelligent Alpha—a worthy wolf and opponent—and Josh wanted to be friends. Friends, adversaries, whatever. He wanted to know the thrill of pitting himself against such a brilliant wolf and winning, or at the very least challenging himself in the process.

Forget all the other bullshit about attraction. He ought to be able to get through to the guy, and if it meant playing up to his obvious infatuation, well he'd do that, too. It would only be this one time, harmless enough.

Josh didn't question the thrill that shot right through the center of his body just then. Or the way his pulse quickened, and his internal heat rose. No, he didn't acknowledge any of those immediate, instinctive reactions as he considered flirting with Hayden Garrett. Nor did he wonder why he was so determined to see him before he returned to New Hampshire for another six months.

All Josh knew was it had suddenly become imperative that he do so.

He jockeyed his way through the curbside crowd until he located Hayden, and stepped right in his path.

The other Alpha sighed, looking very annoyed. "What do you want now, Joshua?" His voice was tight with frustration, his blue eyes icy cold.

Tilting his head up—Hayden had a good four inches on him—Josh gave him his sexiest, most alluring smile.

He was playing a dangerous game, but something inside of him clicked, propelling him forward anyway. It was as if a long-held dam ruptured, carrying Josh along with the raging current and giving him permission to do something risky, new...and possibly insane.

He narrowed his eyes with wolf-like hunger and, gazing up into Hayden's handsome, intelligent face, said softly, "Have a good Christmas, Garrett. Expect a call from me on the twenty-eighth. In fact, you can count on it." Then, with a quick wink, he loped off to his job—his loser, small-town, nothing job.

Yeah, that remark had stung, but he'd never pegged Hayden for a cruel man. So if he'd lashed out, it had been in an understandable need for dominance in a frustrating, vulnerable situation. What Alpha wouldn't do the same? Especially an Alpha who possessed the keen intelligence and self-respect like Hayden did.

Besides, Josh was willing to overlook one verbal barb if it meant he could get through to Hayden. The futures of their packs rested in their hands, which meant it was up to Josh to begin forging a new link with the other pack's heir apparent.

He kept telling himself unity was the only reason he'd practically chased Hayden Garrett across the airport, was why he kept humming holiday tunes to himself with particular enthusiasm. Of course he was pumped. It was a time of year for goodwill to men, and he'd just made the perfect opening gambit for it.

But as he moved bags all afternoon, his nostrils kept burning with those strong scents of arousal and seduction, the ones Hayden had given off like intoxicating, musky cologne. In fact, it almost seemed as if Hayden's powerful wolf scent had permeated his own skin somehow, had woven its way deep into the wool of his sweater and the fibers of his faded jeans and the cotton of his long johns.

While Josh worked and sweated all the rest of the snowy afternoon, he whistled, "I'll Be Home for Christmas", promising himself that his interest in Hayden Garrett was all about peace.

Chapter One

Five years later

Hayden could have just gone ahead and shot himself. At least it would have gotten the torture over with. Butterflies kicked around inside his gut, his heart pounded with expectation, and his palms sweated with the worst kind of dread and embarrassment. No fucking way was this prearranged meeting going to end well. It wasn't even going to happen. The hair along Hayden's nape kept prickling, giving him a bad feeling about the whole set up.

The council elders had decided that drastic measures were called for in order to stop recent escalating violence between the two rival packs in the area. Lately the aggression and marking had breached boundaries, and just last week two males—one from each of their packs—had wound up dead after a bloody brawl. As a result, the elders demanded a peace settlement. That's why they'd arranged this meeting between Hayden, second in line of his own pack, and the secondary Alpha from the other clan.

Hayden was hardly involved with pack policies or

dealings these days, but as heir apparent, he'd shown up as requested. And Joshua Peterson—curse his unreliable, smug ass—was supposed to be here representing his own pack in the exact same capacity. Hayden cringed inside just thinking about seeing the other wolf.

Josh Peterson was literally the last man alive he wanted to face, not about anything and definitely not about the council's current proposition. Now, it appeared Josh didn't even have the balls to show for the sham of a meeting.

Hayden had known the idea sucked from the first moment the council members approached him, suggesting this unique way of brokering peace between the warring clans. "Given your special...situation," they'd said, "we thought this initiative might have particular appeal to you."

Because he was gay he was supposed to roll over and play dog? Supposed to be satisfied with taking a rival and near enemy as a lifemate? Hayden couldn't imagine anything more mortifying than binding himself to a man whom he'd always wanted, but who would never return his own desires and longings. Especially not with as primal and powerful the mating act was between any two wolves, gay or straight. The supernatural bonding linked their souls and bodies together, a process that began during sex and continued to solidify over a period of weeks. Weeks when two literally became knit together as one. Weeks when the sheer power of the connection inhibited the mated pair's ability to transform from human to werewolf.

Hell, no, he didn't want to share anything that intimate or emotional with Joshua Peterson, not now, not ever. Hayden had finally gotten over the damned guy, and he wanted to keep it that way—not talk about some jack-off council member's idea of them mating for peace.

Hayden snorted at the ludicrous nature of the proposition. He was gay, had been sure of it since he was fifteen. Josh, on the other hand, was a strong, brooding alpha male who—although also unmated—probably didn't have a gay hair in his fur. At least not one he'd willingly own up to.

Great, perfect plan, especially given their past. Hayden buried his face in his hands, shuddering at the memory of that horrible December night five years earlier. He shivered at the images flashing through his mind, hating that a spiral of desire shot straight to his cock. He felt it swell, pressing tightly against the rough denim of his jeans, and he shifted slightly in his seat so he wouldn't ache so badly.

Yeah, dude, you're over the guy. Clearly.

He was here for his people, not for Joshua—well, for Josh's people, too, in a strange sense. They were all werewolves, after all, a secret that bound them together, even as it separated their two packs, which was how the council had managed to gain Hayden's participation so far. Because of one simple reason: He believed peace was possible between their clans. In theory, at least, the elders' idea made sense. What better way to bring harmony and unify their packs, than through their younger alpha males bonding to each other? Such same-sex pairings were not entirely unheard of among werewolves, although extremely rare.

So rare, in fact, that Hayden remained single and unmated at almost twenty-seven years old. Joshua Peterson, on the other hand, was a prowler of women, a connoisseur of what lay between their feminine legs. Normally Josh hung in bars just like this one, going on the hunt every weekend. Hayden had sometimes glimpsed him across the way, working his moves, and what he'd observed left absolutely no doubt as to how straight the other wolf truly was.

It was also obvious enough why Josh didn't have a mate himself—he wasn't going to lay down with a female and let himself be claimed or mated. So why in hell did the council think Josh would roll over for any male wolf, Alpha or otherwise?

Yeah, this plan was fucked already. And mortifying as hell. Hayden didn't need his Dartmouth degree to realize what a field day Josh and his pals must be having over this situation. No doubt they'd been guffawing about this meeting ever since it was set up two weeks ago.

Hell, they were probably watching Hayden through the front window even now, observing his nervous binge drinking while patting old Josh on the back. Good work, buddy! He still wants you! Just like he always did, the faggot freak.

Hayden squinted at the large plate glass window at the front of the saloon, but it was too dark to see outside. Now he was becoming paranoid.

Just calm down and get it over with, he coached himself. If Josh didn't show, he would have fulfilled his duty, end of discussion—and knowing Joshua Peterson like he did, Hayden was sure he'd never turn up tonight. Good ole smirking Josh would leave him feeling like a total ass, and laugh about it for the rest of their natural lives.

Hayden buried his face in both hands again, cursing the elders. This mating was a total wet dream for them...and an utter nightmare for him.

A blast of cool air hit his fevered skin, and Hayden glanced up, squinting blearily. Only then did he realize he'd already gotten a bit drunk, but not so wasted that he knew his eyes weren't deceiving him. Oh, yeah, he recognized that confident, graceful stride, as well as the police uniform and stocky build of the man wearing it. He gave a half-hearted wave as Josh approached the back booth Hayden had selected for the meeting.

"Hey, man," Josh said, his voice deeper than it had ever been in the past. His body was bigger and bulkier, too, and they had to adjust the table slightly to accommodate his muscular form. Josh slid into the booth, dumping the contents of his pockets on the table between them—wallet, cop's badge, car keys.

"Not even a hello for an old friend?" Josh asked with a smile, the look in his eerie-light eyes seemingly sincere. The man pulled off a ski cap, raking fingers through hair that still curled slightly despite how short he now wore it.

"You're late," Hayden said sullenly.

Why couldn't Josh have just saved them both the trouble at this point? Hayden stared into his beer, feeling miserable and deciding that he might definitely be halfway drunk.

Joshua flagged a passing server and ordered a Sprite. Then, he turned back to face Hayden, relaxing into the booth seat. "I'm really sorry, buddy. The boss grabbed me for a last minute ride and couldn't get out of it. I hated making you wait."

Hayden met his gaze, tapping his Blackberry. "This never rang."

"I'm not allowed to make personal calls while on duty, Hayden." Josh's eyes narrowed slightly, but he kept smiling. "What, you gonna grill me the whole time or what? I'm here, aren't I? Same as you."

"For this totally fucked-up and fucked-over plan." Hayden shook his head, peeling at the label on his beer bottle.

Josh's expression darkened. "You never used to sound so jaded."

"A lot's happened in my life since...."

"Since we got together last," Josh finished smoothly for him, his expression open and not unkind.

"Yeah, since my innocent youth." Hayden laughed bitterly, staring across the bar.

"I'd hate to see you lose your dreams, Hayden," Josh said gently. "You're the smartest guy in our crowd, with so much potential and talent. Don't get cynical." Josh leaned forward, planting hands openly in front of them.

"Promise me that you won't."

"Why should you fucking care?" Hayden pinned Josh with a hard gaze. He had no clue about all that Hayden had endured since that night five years earlier. If Hayden had become cynical, it was with damned good reason. "Huh? Why should you give a shit what I do or how I live, Peterson?"

Josh's vibrant, lovely eyes never so much as blinked. He stared at Hayden for a long, intense moment, then in an extremely quiet voice said, "Simple, Hayden. Because more than you'd probably believe right now, I do care."

Josh tried hard not to smile at the wide-eyed, bewildered expression on Hayden's face. That look of genuine surprise gave Josh the first real hope he'd experienced for the man since—well, in a very, very long time. The light had gone out of Hayden's eyes years ago. Josh had prayed and waited for it to return ever since.

"I do care," Josh repeated, trying to instill the words with even more intensity. He wanted them to sound like a pledge, and in a very real way, they were. "I care very deeply about you, and about what happens to you, Hayden. Trust me on that one."

But Hayden was dead inside—he had been for so long—and that little spark Josh had glimpsed in his eyes went ice-cold almost as quickly as it appeared. Hayden dropped his head, staring at his beer, fiddling with the label some more—and then tipped the bottle back, draining it dry. Soon as he smacked it down on the table,

Hayden waved at the server, raising two fingers. Was he really ordering two more beers simultaneously?

Josh decided to make a joke of it, hoping he could get Hayden loosened up. "Man, you know double scotch or whiskey is one thing," he teased, "but double Michelob just doesn't have quite the same ring."

"Perfect blend for me," Hayden muttered, drumming his fingers on the table and searching impatiently for the server's return.

So far this little sit-down wasn't exactly meeting the hopeful expectations Josh had maintained before showing up. He leaned back against the booth with a sigh. His back ached like a mother. Too much time hunched at his station desk fooling with paperwork, and when not doing that, stuck in a patrol car. And when not doing that, well, doing things his job required which often left him feeling nauseous and torn up inside. No wonder he hurt all over, right down to his bones.

The server arrived, dropping the two beer bottles in front of Hayden, and he instantly drained more than half of the first one. Josh scowled in concern.

"Hitting it pretty heavy there, aren't you, buddy?" He pointed at the bottles.

"You keeping count?" Hayden lowered his head slightly, narrowed his eyes. Josh would've sworn he even heard a gravelly growl rumble out of the other man's chest.

Yep, Hayden was blitzed, all right. Had to be, if he was posturing so early in the meeting, which made Josh melancholy, almost as if he could feel that hollow place Hayden carried around right inside his own chest. In fact, he was pretty damned certain that he did.

Josh cleared his throat. "I am a cop, you know." He pointed to his badge where it sat between them. "So, drink all you want, but I'll drive you home."

"No. Fucking. Way."

Josh would have decided this meeting was a bust except for one simple reason. He'd come knowing what bad shape Hayden was in, and had no illusions about what he'd be dealing with. Josh was prepared to spend months trying to get through to him—to burrow past the years of heartache and loss and guilt, and make a genuine breakthrough.

According to Hayden's dad, Josh was probably the only one who might still be able to reach Hayden. He'd admitted as much when he'd come out to the house and proposed this arranged mating on behalf of the elders. Josh had listened, his heart practically in his throat, wanting to confess so much in exchange. He'd longed to tell William Garrett about how poisonous powerful secrets can be between two young men, how while they might free one person, they can just about kill the other.

Josh had already made his decision, however. Hayden's father didn't need to learn everything—he knew enough already. The only person in the entire universe who needed to hear the total truth was the handsome, jaded one seated across the table. And Josh would sit in this booth all night if that's what it took to reach Hayden—and the next night, and the next.

"Look." Hayden's head popped back up as if he had suddenly remembered something. "You realize this isn't my idea, right? I mean, you know I had nothing to do with this asinine plan."

Josh took a slow sip of Sprite. "Of course I know that."

"'Cause I don't want you to think I'm still hot for you after all this time...or that I even want this mating. 'Cause I don't. Want you, I mean, not now."

"Hayden, I'd smell the scents, remember?" Josh reminded him gently. "I'm well aware that you fell out of...well, got over..."

"I don't want you anymore," Hayden announced with an almost vicious bluntness.

Of course he didn't think Hayden still held those strong feelings, but to hear it admitted so harshly still tore Josh to the very core. It was as if the other wolf had just slashed open his belly, ripped into him with both jaws, going for the kill.

But why should he expect Hayden to hold back or feel any differently? Josh's womanizing reputation was well known around town. He knew Hayden had seen him frequenting the bars, often with a different woman on his arm. Not only that, but given how things had gone between the two of them in the past—at least how Hayden remembered events—he probably figured Josh would be relieved.

Oh, God, if only he knew. If only he understood all that he doesn't remember. Or what I've been doing all these nights out around town.

There would be time. He would tell Hayden everything at just the right moment, when he was ready. Until then, Josh's only job was to ease Hayden into the proposed mating arrangement and give him the truth slowly. That, and pray that he could regain the man's precious, beautiful trust once again.

Chapter Two

Five years earlier, December 28th

Hayden sat at the family's kitchen table, working on his thesis. There were only three months left for him to complete it, and although that should be plenty of time, the stormy day outside was good enough reason to stay in and work. Dark snow clouds filled the sky, and the sound of distant thunder periodically rolled through the valley.

So much for glimpsing the full moon tomorrow night. Not that it mattered. Josh hadn't phoned yet, and it was already five p.m. At this point, Hayden would've laid money that the promised phone call never would happen. Typical. Joshua Peterson had Hayden's engine all revved up, leaving him with nothing but fantasies and lust once again.

But he'd be lying to himself if he didn't admit that he'd been hovering around the house all day hoping the damned phone would ring. He'd never given Josh his cell number, and didn't want to risk missing him if he went out for a while. Besides, what would his parents say if they fielded a call from Joshua Peterson? There would be way too many questions about why he was suddenly hanging around with the ascending Alpha of their rival pack.

Hayden rubbed his eyes, weary from staring at the computer screen for so many hours. His mom poked her head in the kitchen. "Can't you take a little break?" she asked, her brow knit with concern. "You've been working most of your time home. It would be good for you to get out for a while. Maybe you and your father could go hunting tonight."

"No," he replied, his tone too forceful for such an innocuous question. "No, thanks, Mom," he added more gently. "Don't mean to be jumpy, just...got my mind on stuff."

The kitchen smelled like chocolate cake and fresh-brewed coffee. His mother always spoiled him when he came home for the holidays. "Your thesis?" she asked, wiping her hands on a towel.

"Yeah, that, plus some assignments and research," he lied, glancing over at the silent telephone. He'd wasted almost the entire day staring into space, thinking about Josh, but that was the last thing he'd own up to with her. She knew he was gay, of course, but not pining for an enemy Alpha.

His mother appeared trouble, studying him for a long moment. Did she suspect his real feelings? A wolf herself, she had finely honed instincts.

"Suit yourself, sweetie," she said with a sigh. "I'm concerned about you, that's all. You seem really stressed today."

"I'm fine. Totally fine, I promise, Mom." He thumped his chest. "No need to worry about me."

She went back to the kitchen, and he stared at the laptop screen some more. Maybe his mother was right, and he should get outside on his own. Give up on his pathetic hope that Josh would call about getting together.

He shoved back from the table, stretched and got up to grab a beer. Right as he passed by the phone, it suddenly rang, emitting a shrill, jolting sound from where it was mounted on the wall. And as much as Hayden had hoped the thing would make some sound, any kind at all, he still yelped in startled surprise before yanking the receiver to his ear.

The awakening reaction hit him before the other man even had a chance to speak. It was Josh, his strong force of nature powerful and evocative—even across the telephone line. "Happy holidays, Hay." Josh hadn't used that nickname since their long ago days together on the high school baseball team.

Damn but something about Josh's easy use of the nickname felt intimate, affectionate...as if they were connected by a dozen private threads only the two of them shared.

"Hi, Joshua," Hayden said, casting a nervous glance toward the kitchen. He sure as hell didn't want his mother hearing this particular phone call. "Have a good Christmas?"

They exchanged pleasantries, keeping the conversation light and easy enough, and then after about five minutes, Josh cleared his throat. "Uh, listen, buddy. About tomorrow night...uh, something's come up."

Hayden's eyes drifted shut and he hated the huge swell of disappointment that washed over him. He'd been prepared for this, had figured the plans wouldn't pan out. He braced for the letdown, except Josh kept talking. "Gotta work until about nine," he said. "Yeah, I know it sucks, but let's still meet up then. Cool with you?"

Hayden heard himself make sounds of agreement as if from a distance. The moment had an air of unreality to it, like something straight out of Hayden's crazy daydreams. But, no, they really were going to meet for beers—and go on a run after. His heart did a crazy jackknifing rhythm inside his chest, and his hands began to tremble in anticipation.

"So, here's the deal," Josh continued easily. "I don't have to work the next day. I can stay out late...all night, really. If you're still game for a run, I mean."

Hayden swallowed hard. "Totally. I'll bring a change of clothes."

They decided where to meet, and Hayden hung up the phone, filled with such raw energy, he would've sworn he could bound across thousands of miles in wolf form. Pacing around the table, he reminded himself that Josh was only reaching out as a friend. Yet that thought did nothing to kill his happy buzz. Whatever it meant, tomorrow night with Josh seemed monumental, life-altering.

Chapter Three

Hayden squinted drunkenly at Josh, hating that the other Alpha had only become more stunning in recent years. Although Hayden would never admit as much. Hell, no. The jerk didn't deserve even the slightest ego stroke. Besides, Joshua Peterson's beauty was hardly a newsflash in this town, whether you were male or female, gay or straight.

No wonder Hayden had once been so enthralled with the guy. Hell, he'd have done just about anything to win Josh's affection, but those days were gone. Dead gone. Studying Josh now, all strong and clean-shaven in his cop's uniform, it was obvious how much they'd both changed. They weren't even the same two men they'd been back then.

God, could five years truly be an eternity if enough bad shit went down?

Hayden leaned back in the booth and decided to utilize a method Josh had to be familiar with as an officer of the law. Interrogation. Hell, it was far too fucking familiar to Hayden himself. Lawyers, cops, prison officials.

Interview after interview, question after question. He could play the game in his sleep by now.

"So why did you even show up, Joshua?" Hayden stared down at the other wolf's police ID. "And any particular reason why you dropped your fucking badge between us? Was it to remind me about my past? Or just to make me feel intimidated by you?"

"God, are you really this harsh all the time now?" Josh asked, sliding his badge to the side. "I dropped my shield because it cuts into my thigh if I keep it pocketed. This is a tight space, and I'm just about bursting out of my uniform, as you can probably see." Josh pulled at his uniform collar as if being strangled. "That's the damn thing about what we are, Hayden. Our bodies keep growing and expanding until we hit thirty. Look at how much muscle and heft you've put on. You're even more of a man than before...which is truly saying something."

Hayden refused to have any reaction to that comment. But damn if his hands didn't tremble slightly anyway. He quickly placed them in his lap, hoping Josh hadn't noticed.

Josh shifted around in the booth, continuing. "Tight space, tight emotions—and if you don't mind my using your same bluntness—I wanted to breathe a little without getting a crotch-attack from the load in my pocket. Cool with you, Garrett?"

Hayden barely managed to hold back a reply, even though he would have loved to ask precisely what sort of "load" Sergeant Peterson usually packed in the front of his pants. Instead, Hayden just smiled and said, "So you've still got a sharp and feisty streak. I guess that's good news."

A few years ago, pulling such intense heat from Joshua would have stirred his own strong response. Physical, emotional, an entire chain reaction would've erupted inside Hayden's wolf's body. But that was before the terrible, fated night they shared five years ago—a Christmas memory that changed both their lives forever. Much worse, though, was what came after, those two endless years in prison. Playing the patsy, realizing how fully he'd been betrayed.

No, Hayden wasn't interested in bandying innuendo about with the good cop. He preferred to get right down to business because the sooner they dispensed with the council's fucked up mandate, the sooner he could get away from Josh.

"Look, let's talk about this proposed mating arrangement. You know what the elders are suggesting," Hayden said smoothly. Keep up the interrogation, make him answer the questions, he coached himself. "How would you see it working logistically? You're obviously straight."

Josh kept quiet, maintaining Hayden's gaze with steady, magnetic force, but Hayden wasn't about to be daunted. "Not going to answer?" he asked, hating how bitter his tone sounded. "No? Well, let me rephrase the question for the ladies and gentlemen of the jury. You, Joshua Peterson, are a well-known man about town. All the nearby towns, as a matter of fact. I've seen the evidence with my own eyes, oh, at least half a dozen times. You with your tongue down some hot chick's throat. So how does the elders' plan fit into the equation, you lifemating with a man? With me?"

"I will be completely monogamous if we move forward with the bonding. I can assure you of my intentions." Josh inclined his head with a downright gallant gesture. One that seemed genuine and heartfelt. Hayden grew instantly erect in response, returning an eager salute.

"And those women?" Hayden shifted his hips subtly, trying to get his cock to settle back down. "How do you plan for us to...well, if I can get crass about it, we obviously have to seal our deal at least once for the bond to engage between us. And you know how linked we'll be after that. Always in each other's heads, each other's fur. Shit, like twenty-four seven we'll be feeling the bond."

Josh smiled, blushing a little. "I wouldn't mind."

Hayden rubbed his eyes, looking away. Damn, what was going on here? "Josh, again...you're straight." He looked back at Josh. "You honestly think you can lay down with me one time?"

"I could and will give you whatever you desire in the physical area of our mating," Josh said with touching earnestness, then lowered his voice to husky timbre. "I promise to be as gentle as I am eager."

"Eager?" Hayden repeated, feeling dazed.

Josh gave one firm nod. "Very. I would do everything in my power to satisfy and please you as a mate. And not just once."

An intense rush of adrenaline hit Hayden's face so

hard that his eyes watered in reaction. Josh had blindsided him, left him staggering and shattered deep inside. With one simple comment. He would give Hayden whatever he wanted physically? He'd be gentle and very eager?

Hayden shook his head, fighting intense arousal. "Don't say that," he whispered hoarsely, staring across the bar. He just couldn't meet Josh's gaze, not after he'd given such a vulnerable—and damn it—genuine-seeming pledge. "Josh, don't even say shit like that or make crazy promises you won't keep."He swung his gaze back forcefully, staring the other Alpha down. "Just don't."

"Hayden, please…try and keep an open mind."

"I'm fucking wide open, man."

Josh gave him a grudging smile. "So I can see." Then, Josh grew even bolder, and, reaching for the hand Hayden held gripped around the beer bottle, slowly stroked Hayden's knuckles and then his wrist. "Hay, come on, give me a decent shot here."

"You don't want me. Not really," Hayden said.

"You're making blind guesses," Josh said, still stroking Hayden's hand. "While I'm making promises I intend to keep."

Hayden couldn't help reacting; his eyes slid shut and he drank in all that Joshua's touch did to him, how it brought something long-dead roaring back to life. Or at least it nearly did, if only Hayden would've surrendered to the emotions. Instead, a rush of frustrated fury burst loose inside his Alpha core.

Where the hell did Josh get off trying to be, what? Tender, for God's sake? Hayden jerked his hand out of Josh's reach, lowering his head and growling slightly in threat.

Josh stared down at his own still-extended hand and repeated his earlier words. "Hayden," he whispered again. "Please just..."

"Please, what, Alpha?" he rumbled in reply, rising up out of his seat slightly. "Please mate with you so you can make Daddy a happy man? Don't worry, I know he's got your back against the wall on this one. Or at least that's what I heard."

Josh just stared down at his hands in silence, and then began fiddling with his badge, his brows knit together in heavy concentration. When at last he did speak, he seemed to be choosing his words with extreme care. "There are things you need to know," he said at last, "but I'm not going to blurt them out all at once. This deal with us, Hayden, it needs time. I'm ready, way more than ready...but you need time. So does our relationship."

Hayden jerked back against the wooden booth seat. "What are you talking about? I don't get your whole tone here, none of what's going on. We shared one kiss on that night a long time ago. One quick tussle in the fucking moonlight hardly makes us mating material. One stupid kiss, that's all it ever was, dude."

Josh's cheeks grew flushed. "Well, I've never forgotten it."

Hayden waved him off, growing louder. "Oh, which

part would that be, Peterson? The part where we kissed? Or what came after? When we got drunk and I killed a man out on the highway. Or maybe you remember testifying about how drunk I was—which, by the way, I don't recall since I had the blackout to end all blackouts. Remember that, you motherfucker?"

Josh wouldn't respond, but his eyes filled with stark, obvious pain.

"No?" Hayden reached across the table to shove Josh in the chest. "No? Well I'll tell you exactly what I recall. I wasn't the one driving your truck, and I'm pretty fucking sure that once you wrecked the damned thing, you moved my unconscious body into your seat. You let me take the rap for manslaughter, asshole. You." Hayden waited for a response, but the cop just returned his gaze with cool, stoic calm. "You know, Peterson," he said with a dark laugh, "if that's not betrayal, then I don't know what the hell is."

A long silence spun between them, until even Hayden started to feel uncomfortable, wondering exactly how long Joshua could leave him hanging in the wind on this one. Fine, he'd go whatever distance the other Alpha tried to dictate.

Hayden started looking to flag their server down again, having drained his two latest bottles of beer, when Josh finally cleared his throat. "Hayden, I'm not bullshitting you. All I ask is that you give me time and listen."

"To what, man? The details of how you set me up years ago?"

Joshua scrubbed a hand over his face. "I never set you up. Trust me," he said wearily. "There's just more to all of this than you realize right now. Things I'm working on, a whole lot I want to tell you, but the time has to be right."

Hayden shook his head. No matter how much he would've once welcomed mating with the handsome, guarded wolf across from him, it was impossible now.

"I'm sorry, Joshua, but this plan was fucked from the get go and I can't be part of it," Hayden said. "You should be relieved. You can keep bedding the women, or whatever it is you like to do on your own time, and I'll stay a lone wolf. But this thing with us? It won't work."

He started sliding out of the booth, but Josh grabbed hold of his arm and held on like a manacle. "It was more than a kiss, Hayden. You don't know everything," he said in a forceful, quiet voice. "You have no idea, but it was far more than a kiss we shared, much more than…"

Joshua stopped talking, his words trailing off, fading to nothing. Hayden watched the man's Adam's apple move up and down, captivated by the motion as he waited for him to say more, but no further sound escaped Josh's throat.

More than a kiss? Not possible. Hayden had memorized every detail of the event, the way Josh's tongue felt as it caressed his lips, how strongly their chests had pressed together, the two of them lying in the snow beneath the pregnant moon. Josh had awakened a new hunger inside Hayden's body as his calloused hands cupped Hayden's jaw, drawing their lips together. Then

Josh deepened their shocking and unexpected kiss, truly plumbing the depths of Hayden's mouth as if it were the most important exploration of his life.

With every flick of their tongues, Hayden's desire had spiraled to a crazy height, and for the first time—it had been a miraculous gift—he'd scented arousal radiating off of Joshua. Josh wanted him; Josh was turned on by their single, innocent kiss.

But it hadn't been innocent at all, not once it started. It unlocked an avalanche of cravings and need, and soon there were dozens of erotic aromas wafting between them. Hayden even caught a shocking whiff of Josh's own mating scent as the kiss grew deeper, and they rolled together in the cold snow. Their bodies, so close together, burned with supernatural, lusting heat.

Yeah, Joshua was right—it had been more than just a kiss. More like an explosion, a fireworks showcase, a binding of hearts. Way, way more than a kiss, he would have to agree.

He was going to admit as much, confess to what had awakened inside of him, but when he looked up into Josh's face, he was stunned by what he glimpsed. Those eyes—those gorgeous, magnetic, luminous eyes—were shining with raw emotion.

Hayden had cried after that night, more times than he could count, his heart breaking bit by shattered bit as the full scope of Josh's betrayal had finally become clear in his mind and in the evidence from the car accident. But he never thought to see those same emotions reflected in the other wolf's eyes as he did right now.

A woodsy, tantalizing aroma struck Hayden just then, causing his skin to prickle. He sniffed the air for a moment, unwilling to believe his senses, but then he was sure—Joshua Petersen was emitting the highest possible mating scent. Right here in the bar, surrounded by humans, the guy was radiating the unmistakable marking scent of a werewolf.

Hayden whipped his head around, surveying the rest of the bar to see who had Josh's lust cranked up so high. Surely there was a busty, hard-ridden blonde in here somewhere. Or some auburn-haired biker chick, the sort of woman Josh usually took home after a night in the bar.

Josh's husky, coarse voice answered his unspoken question, electrifying Hayden even more. "It's not some woman," he said plainly. "It's you, Hayden. Ever since then, it's only ever been you."

Slowly, Hayden swiveled back to face the man who'd once been everything his heart longed for—everything his body had desired. He shook his head in disbelief. "That...that can't be true."

Josh rubbed a weary hand across his face, and for the first time Hayden realized how exhausted he seemed. "Why not?" he asked in a heavy voice. "Why would you assume I'm lying? Use your senses. You know what you're picking up. You're getting far more from me than just arousal, aren't you?"

Hayden shook his head, feeling suddenly angry. Josh had always done this, made him feel confined, unable to breathe.

But Josh wasn't done with him yet. "I'll tell you what you scent off me, Alpha," he said in a rough, sexy voice. "You smell my desire. Waves upon waves of it. But you know what's even stronger inside me now? Do you, Hayden?" Josh's eyes lit up, alive with rich amber fire, as if he were being stoked from inside his soul.

When Hayden refused to answer, Josh forged ahead, his voice becoming stronger and more confident. "It's the one you'd most want to deny, but I bet you've caught it...my mating scent. Thick, heavy and full of musk, my aroma's working to entice you. To bring you to me—"

"Never." Hayden snarled at the other Alpha. "You'll never have me heeling to you."

Somehow, Josh remained undaunted, leaning across the table, his eyes bright and alert. "My scent is meant to draw you to my side, wolf to wolf, Alpha to Alpha—and this, for one purpose only." Josh's voice became a rugged growl, his chest rising in short pants. "So that we can join our bodies, coupling together like our ancestors have from the ancient times. Creating that mystical bond that only mates share. That's what you smell coming off me. And it's the very thing I intend to share with you. That the elders request our bonding only makes this meeting easier. More convenient. But I know what I plan to show you, and exactly what I intend to have. You, Hayden. I'm going to claim you."

With that bold announcement, Josh leaned back in the booth, folding both arms over his chest. And then he gave Hayden his familiar smirk, the cocky one that indicated how sure he was that somehow—someway—

Hayden would always belong to him.

All of it unraveled Hayden's cold resolve. He couldn't seem to help himself; he sat up straight in the booth, lifted his nose into the air, and dragged a deep inhalation of the other wolf's aromas into his body.

"My God, Josh," he murmured in amazement. "God, your mating scent, it's gorgeous. It smells...beautiful."

Josh's smile spread, even reached into his eyes. "It's you doing it. You bringing that out of me. You always awakened me, I just didn't understand what you made me feel." He laughed, flushing slightly. "I'm sorry I was clueless for such a long time."

Hayden settled into the booth, narrowing his eyes. "You never knew what to do with me," he said in disbelief. "You laughed about how much I wanted you."

"No." Josh shook his head firmly, straightening his police uniform with a self-conscious gesture. "No, that was never it. It was just...your reaction to me was so intense, so forceful, even when you didn't mean it to be." Josh started smiling again. "You're an Alpha, Hayden, in every way. And when I got around you, I was always...a little shy." He shrugged. "A lot shy, actually. I just wasn't sure how to respond. Not until that night."

Hayden had spent five years telling himself Josh never wanted him, that their kiss had been a drunken fluke. That when they'd become giddy toward the night's end, they had shifted to human form and, feeling overheated from the miles of exertion, fallen into the snow together. They'd still had the beer in their system, were high off their time as wolves, and somehow—even though Josh wasn't gay—he'd cooperated with the kiss Hayden had planted on his lips.

Yet even now, sitting with Josh—feeling his storming desire, hearing his sandpaper voice again—all the lies Hayden had told himself during the time he'd been in prison, all of them seemed to be falling to pieces. No, he couldn't let that happen. Josh had never come to him, not once during those two harrowing years of his imprisonment. Hayden gave his head a clearing shake, determined to cling to his longstanding beliefs about their past together.

"I'm sorry, Joshua, but all of this sounds nice in theory." He released a cynical laugh. "And, yeah, you're juicing up some pretty strong hormones over there, buddy. Not sure how you're doing it, but maybe you're playing tapes of your last one-night stand in your head. No matter what, I'm sorry, I know you're not telling me the truth about what you felt."

"What I still feel," Josh corrected, intense gaze unwavering.

Hayden tossed his hands up in exasperation. "Fine, what you feel—felt—whatever. The point is, I don't believe a word you just said."

Josh's dark eyebrows drew together, and the expression gave him a stern, forbidding look. If Hayden were anything other than Alpha himself, he might have begun backing out the bar's front door. Instead, he waited. Quite patiently, in fact.

Josh spoke in a rumbling vibration. "How can you be sure of what I feel? What gives you the right to say whether I want you or not? Can't you see in my eyes what you've been to me ever since that night?"

"None of that matters. Because I know the truth here, and for whatever reason, you're playing me."

"You tell me what makes you so sure." Josh formed a fist with his right hand, lowering it on the table. The whole booth shook with the quaking force that held Josh in its grip, but Hayden wasn't going to surrender or back down.

"Because if you'd felt anything close to what I did for you," Hayden said, never wavering his gaze. "Anything even approximating what I did...you never would have been able to stay away from me after that kiss."

With that, Hayden slid out of the booth, planted at least sixty bucks on the table between them and said, "Keep the change."

He wondered how far he'd get into the parking lot before Josh trailed after him, insisting on carting him home before he actually did kill someone while drunk behind the wheel. He didn't give his nemesis more than thirty seconds.

Chapter Four

Five years earlier, December 29th

They'd been running together for hours, and even Hayden had to admit he was almost out of steam. Joshua had worked at the airport all day long, so surely he must be about to collapse. They came to a standstill on the rock where Hayden had first seen him three years earlier, and stood side-by-side, tails wagging out their mutual pleasure. For once, Hayden didn't care if Josh was more than a friend or not. The deep, peaceful sense filling his soul was enough. Might even be enough to make him happy from then on.

With a light howl of satisfaction, he lifted his voice toward the moon, singing out his contentment. Josh immediately joined in, his own song a haunting, shockingly mournful one. Then the other wolf nuzzled him affectionately, and for the most infinitesimal moment, Hayden swore he sensed a mating surge ripple between the two of them. Not a physical desire, but a deep knitting between their souls. The impression passed, however, as they continued to lift their voices higher and higher as the clouds parted, revealing the full radiant moon like a prize.

It seemed as if those blissful moments would never end, until with a leap and a giddy yelp, Josh led the way toward his truck, pausing at the low point of the valley. With a keen glance of his rare and gorgeous eyes, Josh seemed to ask him for something—or command him— Hayden didn't actually care. He got the wolf's drift; almost. Almost simultaneously they transformed into their human selves again, and then stood naked and panting in the thick wintry snow.

"Dive in," Josh told him with a nod. "It will cool you down. Then we can move up the embankment and my truck's right there."

Hayden was enthralled. Hypnotized by some sort of spell Josh had woven over him during the past six hours, starting with the beers they'd shared back at the bar. He'd never imagined Josh would let his brusque guard down quite so much, nor express genuine interest in Hayden's college experiences. They could have talked for hours and never run out of things to say.

With a laugh, Hayden fell backward into the snow, and the shocking coldness soothed his fevered skin. Josh lunged down beside him, both of them laughing at the ridiculous image of two grown men rolling naked in the snow. Hayden didn't plan to do what came next; if he had, it would never have happened. But the joy and pure pleasure thrumming inside his veins right then seemed to have only one possible expression.

Hayden reached toward Josh, cupped a hand along his nape, and pulled his mouth closer so he could kiss him. And the word *kiss* was paltry, utterly unable to convey what happened as their lips brushed together and Josh's tongue, shy at first, delved into Hayden's own mouth. All at once, they rolled closer, pulling each other tight. Chest to chest they lay, hearts nearly exploding as one in their wild, hard beating. Josh's sweat mingled with Hayden's, and suddenly their bare hips pushed close together. The cold of the snow beneath them wasn't uncomfortable because they were still exploding with the heat of their wolf nature.

What had begun so gently started to gain the speed of a freight train—each Alpha's core nature battling for dominance, urging him to take the lead. Josh cupped Hayden's face in his hands, dragging him closer to deepen the kiss, and Hayden no longer cared who gained control. He thrust his fingers into Josh's long, curling hair, wanting to inhale him—to lap him up somehow, like water from a stream or to absorb him like stars from the sky itself.

It was the most consuming rush of need and longing that Hayden had ever known. He refused to stop and question whether Josh was leaping in too far or too deep for a straight guy. All Hayden knew was to trust his own heart. Again, they rolled as onc, hips pressing even closer, arms and legs tangled together. Hayden ran his fingers through the damp tangles of Josh's curls, aching to be even closer, wishing it were possible to transcend the barriers of physical separation. Wolf songs echoed through his bones and muscles, penetrated the primitive corridors of his mind.

Josh suddenly pulled back, gasping for air. He had

never looked more gorgeous, and Hayden responded by trailing his thumb along the light beard on his chin and jaw line. "God, Josh, if you knew how long I've wanted this."

Josh smiled, but kept a staying palm against Hayden's bare chest, obviously trying to catch his breath.

Hayden frowned, wondering why Josh had slammed on the breaks. "Too much?" He asked uncertainly, afraid his heart was about to be broken. "Too fast?"

Josh shook his head, raking a shaky hand through his disheveled, damp hair. "Wrong place." He growled as he said it, then grinned at Hayden, a wonderfully suggestive smile spreading across his face. That smile said one thing—Joshua Peterson felt like the biggest, baddest, happiest wolf who'd ever walked open land.

All because of Hayden's kiss.

Chapter Five

Present day

"What'll you do if he doesn't go along with it, Joshua?" his sister Kira asked. She sat in his tiny police station office eating her buffalo burger, waiting for him to finish recounting all the gritty details from the night before. He was lucky his kid sister understood the intricacies of attraction, how sometimes they led you down unexpected paths. She also knew enough to keep all of Josh's secrets—even the darkest, most dreadful ones that were starting to unspool with Hayden.

"He will go along with it." He scowled at her challenge. She just laughed back at his need for dominance.

"But do you have a plan?"

He shook his head. "Only one. The truth...to let everything come out. I am going to be relentless. I know him, sis." He stared out the window, watching the lazy snow falling. "I can get through. What he felt for me—what we felt for each other and we shared...it can overcome anything. Even this."

Kira laughed, taking a bite of her burger. "Well, it certainly sounds confident. And committed."

Hayden smiled, thinking about how clearly he knew what he wanted. Good grief, he'd waited five extremely long years, he sure as hell better know what he wanted by now. His desk phone rang, and seeing it was his commander, he grabbed it off the receiver.

"Hey, boss."

Chief Jenkins was taking a personal day with his wife and kids, so his calling in was to be expected. But it still made Hayden's stomach clutch nervously. What if Jenkins had bad news? What if there had been some change in the case?

"Hey, Peterson, wanted to give you an update on the Rawlings-Keener case." Uh, oh. His boss's voice sounded a bit tense.

"Oh, God, tell me they didn't file a motion or—"

"Hell, no! You're wired tight on this one, Joshua. You need to try and relax a little."

"Doing my best, sir. But you know my personal stake here, and you know how long I worked this particular case."

"Yes, son, I'm well aware of what this one means to you," he said plainly. "You just have to trust things to keep proceeding smoothly."

"So what's the news?"

Josh cleared his throat, looking away from his sister, although he was well aware she was listening to every word traded. She, more than almost anyone, knew how hard and long he had worked to bring this particular case to the grand jury. They already had their indictment—at least that victory had been won. But the next eight months while they waited for the bastards' trial was going to chew his nerves raw.

"They're trying to claim they were set up by the undercover sting."

Josh leaped to his feet. "Bullshit! That's total bullshit!"

"We both know that, but I'm keeping you in the loop. That, and—" Jenkins cleared his throat and the sound crackled over the phone line, "—I have to ask, son. There's no chance you'd be willing to press charges of your own? For what they did to you and..."

Hayden's throat tightened up on him. "Boss, I can't. I told you from the get go. Said I'd take them down, and I did, but my own situation stays out of it. We've got enough without—"

"I understand," the older man said firmly. "I won't ask again. But so long as you know there's a chance this thing could get tossed out. If it does, Rawlings and Keener walk. That's all I'm saying. But what you've got..."

"Is only my word against theirs. No corroborating evidence, nothing." Except the possible testimony of a man who has no memory of what really happened that night. "We both know there's not a case there. It might have been different if I'd come forward at the time."

Jenkins made a chiding sound. "We've already been over that, son. I understand what your motives were."

"Thanks, sir. Keep me posted."

Josh returned the phone to its cradle and stared at it

for a very long time, almost as if he half-expected the inanimate object to give him some much-needed advice.

When he looked away at last, Kira's stare was locked on him, and she was clearly gauging whether or not he wanted to talk about it. He rubbed his eyes and buried his face in his hands. All these promises he was giving Hayden—what if he couldn't back them up? What if the man he loved might still be in danger, even now when Josh had been sure he was finally safe?

"Tell me those freaks don't have a shot at walking," she blurted after a moment, clearly unable to contain her fears. "After what they did to you, Joshua—everything they've done, to so many people—you tell me they won't somehow cut a break or a deal or something." His little sister stared up at him like she used to do when they were much younger, when she was first learning how to shift to wolf form and had been so frightened.

Tell me this won't hurt, she'd almost begged the first time he'd taken her out for a night run, her huge blue-green eyes filled with terror. Her gaze held that same honest need for reassurance right now. She was the gentlest member of their immediate family, the only true Beta in their midst.

He'd placed a heavy burden on her slight shoulders when he'd decided, six months ago, to come clean about why he'd spent three years doing undercover work to bust Edwin Keener and Burton Rawlings. Until then the secrets had been toxic acid, eroding his insides. And even though his bosses knew how personal his stake was in bringing those thugs down, it wasn't the same. He'd needed someone in his inner circle, someone who really loved him, to know why he'd seemingly lost hold of his sanity—and how Hayden Garrett fit into the whole fucked up mess.

"Sis, we both know that sometimes cases go south," he said. "Dad saw it happen in his job. You remember."

They'd grown up with a father who was a police officer, just a hardworking, good man, who had finally retired to focus on leading their people.

"You're not promising me they're going to get what they deserve," she said.

Her kind gaze never moved from his face, and it touched him how much she cared. And that she hated those two men almost as much as he did—maybe even more because they'd hurt her big brother.

"Kira, sweetie," he told her gently, "I put together the best evidence I could. I think it's all going to be fine. We made it past the grand jury, a huge hurdle."

She nodded, picking at her burger. He decided to lighten things up. "So, let's get back to the really juicy, good stuff. My love life."

Kira laughed, her freckled nose crinkling. "You are so demented."

"No, I'm a highly focused individual."

She made a playful, wolfish snarl. "Alpha. You are so, so totally Alpha, it's not even funny. I hope Hayden's into that."

This really made him laugh. "Good grief, do you remember Hayden? How flipping Alpha he is? I'm downright docile and Beta compared to him." He smiled, thinking of how many times he and Hayden had circled each other over one issue or another. Right now, things between them sure felt hopeless, but maybe—just maybe—it was simply more of their Alpha natures battling for dominance.

Kira's smile slipped away and she became serious again. "I hate to ask this, Josh, but what if Hayden won't forgive you? For all that you kept from him...well, all of it?"

Josh wiped his hands definitively. "I cannot allow myself to consider the possibility." Josh rolled his desk chair back and checked his watch. "I'm picking him up in an hour."

"Does he know you're coming over?"

He gave his sister a playful wink. "Nope, or he probably wouldn't be there."

"Joshua. I'm not so sure this non-plan of yours is the best one you've ever come up with."

"No, it really is. And heading over to Hayden's place now is perfect for phase one."

She didn't appear totally convinced and gave him a skeptical half-smile. "I see."

"For real! In fact, my strategy's going to tear down all the cynicism he's hiding behind." He smiled, thinking of what the situation required. "You see, sis, I'm going to woo him. Day by day, I'm going to win his heart back."

She cleared her throat. "Sweetie, uh, not to be a killjoy, but you know," she said, "Hayden may not even open the front door when he sees it's you."

"He will."

"And you know this how?"

"I just do." Josh leaned down and kissed Kira on the cheek, then glanced in the small mirror he kept on his office wall. With a quick sweep of his hands, he made sure his hair was neat and smoothed out his uniform. When he caught Kira's gaze, she seemed to be waiting for a better explanation.

With a sigh, he leaned against the edge of his desk. "Because one night, a long time ago, Hayden Garrett fell in love with me. He gave me his heart...his very soul. And I gave him all of myself, too. He just doesn't remember it. Not yet."

"Good luck!" His sister called as he bounded out the door, hardly able to contain the thrill he felt about seeing Hayden.

Oh, God, let it work, Josh prayed, practically vaulting down the office stairs and to the first floor.

Hayden lay in the middle of his king-size bed, staring at the ceiling. The same thing he'd been doing for hours, and none of his thoughts made any more sense than they had while he'd tossed and turned for most of the night. It didn't help that his sleep cycle was twisted like a misshapen pretzel. He would be working again tonight, like he always did, grooming the ski slopes over at the resort. Work all night, sleep all day. Until he'd seen

Joshua again, the schedule had suited his dark moods perfectly.

Just scraping by, barely existing. Perfect self-imposed punishment for crimes he supposedly committed, yet had no memory of. And even though he suspected he hadn't been driving the night of the car accident, he still deserved to burn in hell for the huge way he'd fucked up all the expectations his folks had pinned on him, their only child.

He wasn't sure if rage or confusion was causing his immediate turmoil. After the stunt Josh had pulled in the parking lot of the bar last night, Hayden had wanted to slam him against his fucking police cruiser. The man had the balls to follow him out to the car and swipe his keys. As if that wasn't bad enough—he wasn't honestly going to drive, for God's sake. He'd planned to call a taxi, but then Josh had forced him into the back of the cruiser like he was some common criminal.

They'd shouted and postured there in the lot, and Hayden had definitely been drunk. Drunk enough that he'd come within an inch of fulfilling that vision of slamming Josh violently up against the car. Only that image had dissolved too quickly, replaced by a much stronger desire to shove the cop against the vehicle and kiss him senseless. To push the man down onto the hood and mount him, public viewing be damned.

He hadn't exactly been thinking on his feet, had he? It had been embarrassingly easy for Joshua to shove him in the back seat of the car and lock him in.

"Oh, great, buddy." Hayden had draped his arms over

Josh's seat, leaning into the front part of the car. "This is doing wonders for my already extremely tarnished reputation. Last thing I need around this two-bit town is for people to see me being driven home in a police car."

Josh hadn't answered, keeping his eyes straight ahead on the snow-covered road.

"What happened to all the shit you were talking back inside the bar, huh?" Hayden had asked, voice a little too loud. "About you making me see the truth of things?"

Josh had turned toward him then, just for a moment. Long enough for Hayden to feel the warm familiarity of his scent; how was it possible that any man could smell so damned delicious and alluring while being such a jerk?

"I'm taking care of you, Hayden," he said simply. "That's what a mate does."

He'd popped Josh in the shoulder. "We're not mated, you freak. In fact, we're not even gonna talk about it anymore."

"Yes, we are." The calm confidence in Josh's statement had stilled Hayden for a moment.

"Yes we are..." What? Talk about it? Do it? "We are what?" he'd finally mumbled, feeling the many, many beers hit his system hard.

Josh kept silent, and then his police scanner erupted in chatter. Josh instantly silenced it, turning off the highway toward Hayden's small house.

"You know where I live?" Talk about an embarrassing thought. His little shack of a home was shockingly modest. As often as his parents tried to offer him money

71

for a fresh start, he refused to accept it.

"I know a lot about you, Hayden," Josh told him quietly. "I've kept my eye on you all along. Like I said."

Hayden sank back against the seat, feeling exhausted. More tired than he could remember feeling in a long time. With shaking hands he tried to neaten up his too long hair. Whereas Josh kept his naturally dark curls trimmed short these days, Hayden had grown his own wavy brown hair to his shoulders. It allowed him to be anonymous at his resort job, like every other ski bum employed at the place, not like a twenty-seven-year-old Dartmouth graduate and former inmate. One who sure as hell should've been doing something important with his life by now.

He rubbed his eyes, trying to understand all the crazy shit Josh had hit him with tonight. And then one thought surfaced, one that disturbed him most of all.

"So, Josh," he ventured, "if you cared so much, then I don't get why you never came to see me. You were never at the hospital, didn't show up on visiting days during my two years of hell, doing time."

"You don't know what happened when you were in a coma," Josh interrupted quietly. "Those six weeks are a blank, your father told me."

"You never came. I'd have known," he said bitterly. "And you definitely never came while I was in prison. I kept waiting. Some dumbass part of my heart really thought you'd bring a cake and we'd make jokes about you hiding a file in there. I waited...man, I was nuts then." He settled back against the seat, rubbing his eyes. Yeah, he'd been naïve enough to hope Josh might show. For a while.

"I'm sure it must've been hard to understand why I didn't visit you," Josh answered in an even tone. "But you have to trust me, Hayden. I had my reasons, and they were...."

Hayden lurched forward, leaning over the bench seat so he could be closer to Josh, could force him to finish the sentence. "Tell me what they were," Hayden demanded, grabbing the other man's forearm. "Tell me they were good. Worth what you did to me."

For a brief moment, Josh reached over and covered Hayden's hand with his own, letting it rest there, the warmest kind of contact. "Rock solid reasons. If you can trust me, even a little, I will make you understand what they were."

Hayden shook his head. "Can't trust you, dude. Not now."

Josh squeezed his hand, and the gesture felt like pleading. "Hayden, please."

"If you give me one 'rock solid' reason, I'll consider the possibility."

Josh nodded, let his hand drop and stared at the road ahead. He drew in a heavy, long breath and said, "You won't believe this, at least not yet, but I was protecting you. In fact, I was willing to give up everything in order to keep you safe."

"From whom?" Hayden began laughing. It was the last

and lamest excuse he ever would've imagined. "Who in hell did I need protection from...other than you?"

Josh never answered, just grew extremely quiet and then turned up the police scanner. They didn't speak again until he pulled into Hayden's long driveway. Then, getting out of the car, he opened Hayden's door and walked him toward the front of his extremely modest house. God, how he hated Josh to see the low-rent digs he called home. Here he was, the former golden boy living in a fishing shack. At least the place was remote enough that nobody would see him being carted home in a police car.

For a moment, they stood there at the front door as if—yeah, right—they were going to share a goodnight kiss. Joshua stepped to the side while Hayden unlocked his door, and then as Hayden entered, Josh was right on his heels. It was dark, and he couldn't see what happened, but he certainly felt it. Josh's muscular, solid arms came around him from behind, pulling him close. For a long moment he stood, his back to Josh's chest, listening to the rise and fall of their breathing, feeling the manic beat of Josh's heart against his back. And then, with the most tender gesture imaginable, Josh brushed Hayden's long hair off his nape and placed a gentle, chaste kiss there, rubbing his fingers along the cordons of muscle that were tight from long-standing tension. And then he kissed the spot again, just letting his lips brush back and forth with a soothing, tender pressure.

Josh worked those strong hands low along Hayden's abdomen, rubbing, stroking, his circular motion moving dangerously low. "I'm not going to stop coming around, Hayden," he whispered in a husky, thick voice, brushing another kiss along the back of his nape. "You need to know my intentions toward you. So let me be clear, Hay. The council's mandate gives us thirty days to decide if we're willing to mate, but I'm not on that timetable. I'm not on any timetable but yours." Josh paused, waiting, rubbing a thumb across Hayden's right hip. He was poised as if stalking a prey, yet simultaneously seducing Hayden as if he were his cherished, his beloved.

Then, Josh moved his lips against Hayden's right ear, whispering in a low, vibrating tone that sent chills across Hayden's entire body. "I'm a hunter by nature, persistent by bloodline. You better get used to the feel of my arms around you and my body against yours." The muscled arms slid low about his hips, rocking him backward with a shocking, electric motion that absolutely set fire to Hayden's groin. "Get used to this, to me," Josh murmured roughly. "Because, Garrett, you should know... I'm only getting started."

And then Joshua released him, stepping backward without another word. Hayden spun to face him, shock and arousal rippling through him like an earthquake, but the cop was already out the door.

About one p.m. Hayden finally rolled over in bed and groaned aloud. My stupid car, he cursed to himself. It was still sitting back over at the bar, and Officer Helpful had his keys. Or did he? Maybe he'd dropped them on the table by the front door. But Hayden didn't remember Josh having time to do anything like that, not with the way he'd hauled him into that strong embrace and—shit, just held him. So fiercely, and yet with all the tenderness of an intimate lover.

Suddenly, Josh's words from last night whispered in Hayden's mind. *It was more than a kiss.*

Hayden had assumed Josh was referring to the knee-knocking, soul-searing nature of their one, very particular kiss in the snow. Was it possible that more might have happened between the two of them on that fated night, before they'd gotten into that car accident? Hayden pressed his eyes shut, a bright burst of light erupting behind his eyes. Whenever he tried to remember anything after the kiss, his head always felt like it would split wide open.

But as he replayed their embrace from last night, the way Josh had wrapped him close—and from behind, no less—it made Hayden wonder if there might have been something more intimate once they'd climbed into the truck that night, before they'd hit the road.

Rolling onto his back, Hayden trailed fingertips along his belly, imagining that they were Josh's warm, calloused hands. Picturing those rough fingertips dipping low into his boxers, easing the elastic waistband down his hips. Hayden arched slightly, mirroring the actions he fantasized about Josh doing. Slowly, with the same tenderness he imagined Josh would use, he brushed his boxers low down his upper thighs, allowing his pulsing erection to pop free. His arousal fell against his abdomen, thick and hot, and he pictured Josh's hand reaching to hold it.

Oh, and then Josh would take those same coarse fingers, would wrap them around his tip and begin a steady, urgent motion. Slow at first... Hayden lifted his hips, thrusting upward... but then Josh would take command, would turn that friction into something frantic, an expression of all that the other man wanted from him.

He closed his fingertips, working them back and forth about his length, absolutely aching for it to be Josh's hand that was stroking him now. He recalled Josh's tingling, seductive kisses against his nape last night, bucking in pleasure, yearning for the other wolf with a blazing intensity he'd refused to acknowledge for years now.

And then a shuddering flash of Josh filled his mind, naked beside him, his green-gold eyes narrowed and hungry, his lean body gleaming with sweat and power. Oh, yes, baby, he wanted to scream. Yes, I'll accept the elders' plan. For a taste of you, any, yes, I'll do anything.

"Yes," he barked, his warm seed spurting into his hand, his hips hammering off the bed with every spasm of his cock. "Yes! God, yes...." The slick wetness on his fingertips reminded him of what he'd always wanted from Josh—to bring him to orgasm, to come together with him, mixing their male essence in an erotic statement of unity.

To mate. Oh, God, wasn't that what he'd always secretly wanted with Josh?

He kept rubbing his shaft, even after it softened, spreading that slickness across his balls, pretending it was Josh that was touching him. Loving him. Hayden collapsed against the sheets, the coolness of the material a sharp contrast to the heat in his body.

Pressing a forearm over his face he cried out, "Why can't I remember?" What if Josh had been telling the truth last night; what if it hadn't been more subterfuge? If there were parts of that night that were crucial, something before the accident, then it would mean that Josh might never have betrayed him. It could explain how there was so much alcohol in his system, even though according to his memories, they'd finished drinking at least four hours earlier.

Wiping his slick hand across the sheets, Hayden bolted upright in bed. If all of that was possible—if Josh's earnest, shocking pledges from last night had truth to them—then Hayden would have to reconsider everything from a totally new angle. And he really did mean everything—including one sweet kiss that had rocked his world.

Chapter Six

Five years earlier, December 30th, early a.m.

Climbing back into the truck was an exercise in the willing and the equally willing winding up in a tangled heap. Hayden had honestly intended to pull his clothes back on as soon as they got to the vehicle. His libido was already halfway down the highway en route to Josh's place. Surely he could tap his foot in sexual frustration long enough for them to actually get there.

But that admirable plan fell apart as soon as they wound up in the truck together, naked and still gleaming with sweat. Particularly because it seemed that Josh wasn't inclined to wait long enough to drive home.

One minute Hayden was yanking his jeans over his feet, reaching for his sweatshirt, and the next Joshua practically pounced on top of him, tearing the jeans back off. With his natural wolf's grace, Josh slid onto his knees, spreading wide as he mounted Hayden. Hayden swore he saw stars for a minute, he really did, because naked and pressed right up against him was Joshua Peterson exactly as he'd always dreamed of seeing the man. Naked, beautifully aroused, and with his strong thighs open around Hayden's hips.

Josh nestled atop him, brushing tangled, damp hair out of his own face. "I can't drive, not like this," the hot, panting wolf murmured with a shake of his head. "I'm too fucking turned on. Nobody's around anyway. No way I can drive, man. I want you too damned much to go anywhere."

Hayden was speechless. Josh was just so fucking gorgeous, with the moonlight spilling through the window and across his dusky bare skin. Gorgeous and aggressive, such a total turn on for a fellow Alpha.

Josh worked to balance himself. He splayed calloused hands against Hayden's bare chest, already trying to tease himself into a rhythm of sorts. Only he wasn't far enough down onto Hayden's lap to make that work very effectively, so his cock pushed into Hayden's abdomen with every one of his motions. Josh kept moving his strong hips, thrusting and trying to shift lower against Hayden's groin, but the awkwardness of the truck made the whole thing far too difficult.

Hayden didn't even give a damn. Josh was too magnificent, with his thickly muscled body, those dark silky hairs covering his chest and arms and legs. So masculine, very much like the wolf he'd been only a few minutes ago. Hayden loved every gyration of Josh's hard, beautiful body. That Josh was sleek with sweat, his cock hard as a plank—poking Hayden in the belly with every small movement he attempted—all of it was almost enough to bring Hayden to orgasm already. Unable to hold back, he even made a growling sound of keen pleasure, and that only seemed to tease Josh into more of a sexual frenzy.

They kissed for a moment, mouths desperately opening, tongues swiping and swirling until Hayden couldn't hold back another soft moan. The noise caused Josh to press harder against him, and to release a louder cry of his own. Hayden answered by sliding a hand behind Josh's neck, pulling him closer, for a rougher, more commanding kiss. Their aggressive natures began making demands, back and forth, in the way they touched and explored each other.

Josh gripped Hayden's shoulders, his fingers digging into the bare flesh, and settled his hips down a bit lower. Those powerful thighs of Josh's opened wider, spreading, allowing more intimate contact, and their abdomens brushed together. Their muscled chests pushed and gave, until Josh paused for a moment, staring down into Hayden's eyes. Sharp frustration filled those luminous depths—Hayden understood instantly. This was a straight man—well, maybe not so much—but still. That was the issue. Josh was used to knowing exactly how to go for the gusto and score a home run. Trying to tangle together with another man, probably for the first time in his life— while wanting that same man with an almost painful intensity—it was messing with the Alpha's need to take charge.

Hayden smiled, getting it completely. For a long, slow moment, he leaned back against the seat and just looked up at Joshua in awed admiration. The man was a rare thing of beauty at that moment. All breathless, overheated, and ripe with mating scents.

Hayden brushed Josh's sweaty curls out of his face, and started to laugh at the craziness of the entire situation. He had this man, the one he'd wanted for years now, bearing down on top of him, and they couldn't seem to get a decent position going, couldn't even figure out the best way to just blow each other. Not with Joshua humping him like he was a woman, Hayden thought, barely stifling a bark of laughter.

As crazy-fevered as they both were, it seemed like the two of them couldn't quite pull the whole thing off, at least in terms of positioning. Hayden cupped Josh by the hips, stilling his instinctive gyrations. Josh frowned down at him, appearing confused and a little... well, shy, surprisingly enough. That disconcerted expression on such a tough, masculine face nearly did Hayden in, then and there.

Josh arched his back, never letting go of his hold on Hayden's shoulders, and leveled him with a dark, erotic gaze. "Don't you want this?" he asked throatily, squeezing his thighs tight against Hayden's legs. Josh dipped his head low and gave Hayden a long, deep kiss, working lazy fingers through Hayden's hair in a kind of caress. Then, Josh's tactic changed, and he tangled those locks within tight, greedy fists, expressing every bit of sexual frustration that Hayden shared with him at the moment.

Waiting to get back to Josh's place instantly ceased to be a viable option.

"Yeah, settle on me, baby," Hayden murmured, eyes drifting shut in the deepest pleasure. Josh straddled a little wider and lower, and bingo, liquid fire speared right through Hayden's groin. "Like that, Josh. Oh, yeah, just like that."

Hayden slid a hand between their abdomens, taking Josh's swollen erection within his own shaky hand. As he enclosed the tip within his fingers, Josh released a low-pitched, aggressive growl. Hayden had never wanted anything so much in his life as to bring this strong Alpha wolf to release, to make the man throw back his head and howl to the fucking moon he was so damned over the edge.

But Josh's earlier words skimmed through Hayden's dreamy, half-aware mind. Not the right place.

"Not the right place," Hayden mumbled, but Josh would have none of that. He clasped Hayden's jaw, dragging his mouth upward for a forceful, demanding kiss. Hayden shook his head again, protesting weakly. He was the one with experience in this department—at least, that's what he'd thought until the last few minutes. This first time had to be incredible for Joshua; in fact, it was supremely important to Hayden that he take him to realms of pleasure no female lover had ever dared show him—or ever could—before this night.

Josh cocked his head, studying him quizzically, his chest rising and falling with quick, wolf-like pants. "Why not?" he demanded bluntly, forcing Hayden to still the motion he was working over Josh's thick cock. The man was nothing if not beautifully direct, and now that they were getting together, that fact no longer annoyed Hayden. It made him quiver even harder with lust.

Hayden slid his hand down Josh's thigh, stroking it long and slow. Just like he might if Josh were in his wolf form and Hayden were trying to soothe or steady him with his human hands.

"Seriously, man," Josh asked, eyes glazed with desire. "Why not do it here?"

"Because, it's what you said...." Hayden tried to slow his heart's outrageous tempo. "Not... the right place. Not for the first time."

Josh nodded, sexual frustration and impatience lining his lightly bearded face. Still, he didn't budge, didn't so much as move a muscle to dismount from his intimate position atop Hayden's lap.

"I need to know something," Hayden asked after a moment of them trying to bring their respective bodies under at least a little control. With a long, slow stroke he rubbed Josh's back, loving the way the muscles rippled beneath his hand in reaction.

Josh met his gaze and that downright mystical color of his eyes grew a little brighter somehow. "Sure, anything," Josh said. Then, he laughed a little, that familiar grin turning up the edges of his mouth. "Anything for you, babe." And then Josh really started laughing like a mad man over that stupid line.

Judging by the crazy laughter, Hayden was pretty sure the guy was experiencing a sudden bout of nerves. It didn't help matters that Josh was sitting high and pretty right in the lap of a long-term rival. A rival who just so happened to be a man. Probably Josh's first male lover.

Hayden felt a wave of tenderness wash over him, a strangely protective urge to make sure Josh was comfortable with the whole thing. Reaching up, he brushed an unruly lock of dark curls away from Josh's face, just staring into his eyes. "You've never been with a guy before, have you?"

Josh turned away, staring out the window, but Hayden caught his chin, forcing him to face the question. Once they were looking into each other's eyes, Hayden tried again. "Joshua. Please. If we're gonna do this, I need to know... it's kind of important, actually. Have you ever been with a guy, you know, like this? Made love with one?"

Josh's dark eyebrows furrowed together, and he stared at Hayden's chest for a few seconds. Then, as if resolved, he smiled and looked up. "I'm glad you're going to be my first."

Hayden wrapped his arms about the other man and, shivering with more desire than he'd ever known in his life, whispered, "I'm going to blow your mind, baby. It's going to be so sweet, just you wait." Hayden smiled, already imagining how long and slow he was going to take things with Josh, how gentle he'd be this first time. "And it won't be like any woman you've ever had in your life."

Josh laughed, burrowing his face against the top of Hayden's head; his entire body trembling and shuddering. "Of course not, you sexy moron," he said in a deep voice filled with nervous, fevered excitement. "It's going to be you."

Chapter Seven

Present day

Josh raked a hand over his hair, neatening it for about the twentieth time since leaving the station. Damn, but he wanted to look as handsome as he could for Hayden. Wanted to do something, anything, to recapture the man's attention—he wanted to evoke those same eight or nine scents Hayden used to exude whenever Josh came around. Those musky smells had been like the color spectrum to Josh during their last time together.

Those twenty-four hours five years ago had been the most rapturous ones he'd ever known in another person's arms. It was a man's body that Josh had been born to pleasure, born to explore, created to experience. Or, more specifically, Hayden Garrett's body fit together with his own as if the two of them had been created for no other purpose than joining physically—and their souls for no other reason than mystical union.

Josh rubbed his face, working to tame his aroused emotions. Here he stood, in front of Hayden's door, and he was already in a lather, ready to pounce on a guy who didn't even share the same memories he did.

But he will. You'll awaken them inside of him. He will know the truth.

That hope was all that had kept him going to this point. That, and waiting until Hayden was ready. According to the man's parents, he was as ready as he'd ever be, slipping into a darker and darker place with every passing month. And with Hayden finally out of danger, Josh's long-awaited moment had arrived.

He tucked in his shirt once more, cleared his throat, and with a mixed sense of anticipation and terrible anxiety, banged on Hayden's door.

The seconds ticked off, Josh cleared his throat again, staring at the ground. And by the time a minute or so had passed, Kira's words about Hayden not opening the door for him were ringing in his ears.

"Come on, Hay," he whispered softly. "Open up, buddy. It's me. Open up for me."

Open up your heart to me—open up that brilliant mind of yours and just remember.

After more than five minutes had passed, Josh's cop instincts started doing a spastic jig across his chest, whispering that somehow, someway, Keener and Rawlings had sent someone after Hayden. That they'd reached beyond the confines of prison, targeting the one person Josh had leveraged his very soul to protect against their particular brand of violence.

First Josh walked around the back of the property, looking for anything that might seem suspicious. A broken window, an open door, a discarded weapon. He did so by using his cop instincts, but his wolf instincts were right in there, too, nearly going berserk. His arms and legs tingled, the feeling that always signaled he was about to turn wolf. But as soon as he'd subdued that aspect of his transformation, soft fur began covering his chest and abdomen, itching horribly beneath his uniform. He was out of control, hardly able to prevent the strong wolf inside of him from emerging.

If anything had happened to Hayden—if Keener or Rawlings had sent someone to harm him—Josh would forget working on the side of law and order. He would hunt them and anyone they cared about down, and show them the true meaning of raw, cold power. Hayden was his, a part of him, and he hadn't sacrificed so many years with the man for any enemy to snuff out his life.

The thought of losing Hayden finally did Josh in. He ripped off his clothes and bounded into the woods just behind Hayden's house, his strong, heavily-muscled legs already transforming and realigning their shape, his posture changing, his entire nature becoming that of an Alpha mate, protector to his very marrow. That it was daylight and dangerous for such a transition, Josh never even counted the cost. His instincts catapulted him, drove him to ensure Hayden's safety, and once his change was complete, he leaped up onto the small wooden deck along the back of his lover's home. Sniffing, moving like the natural born predator he was, he released a rumbling, furious sound.

Then, bounding onto a rickety table on Hayden's deck, he used his heightened vision to gaze through a small window. He studied the home's interior, searching for anything that might indicate foul play. Neither his sense of smell, nor his vision, gave him cause for alarm, but he couldn't seem to bring his own fears to heel. Nudging at the window, he realized it was unlocked and slightly open. Panicked to find it that way, Josh steeled himself against whatever pain he was about to experience, and leaped at the glass window with all the supernatural force in his body. Smashing through, he landed in the middle of the kitchen, ignoring the scent of his own blood, and began prowling farther into Hayden's home.

A towel wrapped about his hips, Hayden walked into the kitchen, a man on a hunt. Not for elk or deer, as he would on a full moon, but for the coffee pot. His head felt like it was about to split in half, the headache that had begun earlier now beating at his temples like a jackhammer.

His long hair was too wet, rivulets of water rolling across his chest and down his pectorals, all the way to his abdomen. He loosened the towel from about his hips and brought it to his head. Bending over, he rubbed the towel back and forth in a rough motion, working the dampness out. Once done, he wrapped it about his neck and continued toward the coffee pot, not caring that he was naked. It was natural to him, being unclothed, as it was for all of their kind. It wasn't like he'd take off to the resort in the buff, but he felt at ease moving about his home without even wearing his boxers.

Dumping out the day-old coffee, he scrunched his

nose at the gross scent, then rubbed at his nostrils in an effort to clear them. What hit him next made him whip around with a growl. The strong odor of blood. Wolf's blood.

"Who's here?" he demanded, dropping into a crouch. A quiet whimper answered, followed by a rumbling wolf's lament.

Lifting his nose into the air he knew instantaneously that Josh was in his house—in wolf form—and injured.

He was a first-class idiot, Josh decided of himself. He was sprawled back in Hayden's bedroom, reeking of blood and unable to shift back to human form. Yeah, way to make a great impression on the man you love, he thought, whimpering out his frustration.

Dropping his nose onto his paws, he hoped like hell that Hayden wouldn't decide he was the most possessive, smothering Alpha mate ever to exist. Hayden needed time and space, so what did he do? Behaved like a moron and did the most half-cocked, stupid thing any werecop had ever contemplated. At least he could take solace in the fact that he was possibly the only werecop currently employed by any law enforcement division on planet earth, so at least there wasn't a lot of competition for the title.

A gentle, strong hand touched the top of his head, and Josh jolted. Hayden knelt beside him, and stroked his face, his ears. "You nutcase," he said gently, continuing to pet him with soothing strokes. "You broke through my kitchen window, didn't you?"

Josh nuzzled against Hayden's side, panting from the exertion and the painful cuts and bruises that abraded his right side and flank. Hoping Hayden would hear the apology in his tone, he released a whining sound, begging forgiveness for being such an ass.

Hayden bent his face low, nuzzling him back, tickling and rubbing his ears. "Okay, well, you asked me to trust you last night," he said. "Now you gotta trust me, buddy. Let me take care of these cuts."

Josh watched as Hayden stood and walked away, and definitely appreciated the gratis view he got of that naked, lean and outrageously beautiful body of Hayden's. Except, curse the dumb luck, he'd gotten the peep show while unable to transform into human form. If he had been able to, then the entire going slow and wooing plan would have been shot to hell.

He wouldn't have been able to hold back, not after the stunning view Hayden had given him of abdomen muscles that rippled with strength, narrow hips, and much broader shoulders. Josh had seen a lot of his fellow male wolves before and after they made their change, but he'd never glimpsed a man more gorgeously sculpted than the one who'd just left him in this fit of sexual frustration. Even the stingy cuts along his fur-covered body didn't do much to dampen his longing. With a growl, he managed to rise onto all fours and leap into the center of Hayden's big bed. Might as well send the guy a message when he returned to tend to his wounded ego—and body. At the moment, he didn't know which one felt more banged up.

"Well, this was an interesting beginning to day number two." Hayden never looked up from the laptop where he worked, his fingers still poised over the keyboard.

Josh felt off-kilter and a little woozy. Probably because he'd knocked his head pretty hard when he'd gone smashing through the window. Now he stood in Hayden's living room, rubbing his temples, glad he'd been able to assume human form again. He couldn't afford to waste a moment, not with all he wanted to make Hayden understand.

He padded along the rug, Hayden's sweatpants dragging with each step. Nothing like putting on a much bigger guy's clothes to make you feel like a total wuss. Like you weren't nearly large enough to compete Alpha to Alpha. Then again, the T-shirt Hayden had left on the bed was almost too tight across his chest. Their bodies were just different, plain and simple, and it was part of what turned him on so much about Hayden.

"Day two, huh?" he asked groggily, still rubbing his throbbing temples. "You keeping count now?"

"The council gave us thirty days to decide," Hayden said, never looking up from his work. "I'm just clocking time, man."

Hayden had seemed so open when Josh was wounded and panting at his feet, downright tender in his ministrations. Now? Well, the barriers were clearly back in place, as was his requisite cynicism.

"I already told you," Josh said firmly, "I'm not on the council's timetable. Besides, I know what I want, and I'll wait long as it takes."

Hayden's entire posture stiffened, as if he'd just caught an unknown scent on the wind. He even tilted his chin upward. Then he leaned back over his keyboard. "What you want?" he asked, a hint of flirtation in his tone, even if he wouldn't look up and meet Josh's hungry gaze.

"Who I want. Is that precise enough for you, Garrett?" Josh was shocked by how husky and lust-filled his own voice sound.

Hayden clearly noticed the sensual tone because he turned in his chair, finally meeting Josh's own fevered gaze with a sexy smile. The only real smile that he'd seen on Hayden's face in years. Then Hayden noticed Josh's mis-sized clothing, his eyes widening in amusement as he took in the sight. "Oh, man," he snorted. "Now that's just hysterical."

"Okay, have your fun." Josh folded arms over his chest, nodding his head. "Go on. I'm the short guy, the stocky little Alpha. Have your laugh at my expense."

Hayden began laughing even harder. "I'm sorry...seriously, you are..."

"Short." Josh's face burned and he grinned at the floor. "Like I said, have your fun. I deserve it after that stunt with your window."

Hayden waved him to silence. "No, I was going to say that 'short' is like the last thing I'd ever say about you."

Hayden turned all the way around in his chair, a disbelieving expression on his face. "You really are kidding, right? 'Stocky little Alpha'?"

"You've got at least five inches on me."

"I doubt it."

"By the way, used to be four. I calculated." Josh walked closer and sat on the other side of the table from Hayden. "But damn if you didn't keep growing, you sneaky bastard. Even more than I did. You must be a solid six-feet-six now."

"Which makes you six-feet-one, Peterson. Only an Alpha would ever consider that height 'stocky.'"

Josh laughed. "Well, compared to a big Alpha like you, Hay, I do feel short."

Hayden averted his eyes, his face flushing visibly. "Are you saying...you like my size?"

"You have a body that's just made to be worshipped," Josh murmured reverently, unable to keep his feelings on the matter to himself.

"Funny," Hayden replied slowly, as if considering the matter. "That's exactly what I always thought about your body. Hotness incarnate, I remember that's how I used to think of it." Hayden drew circles on the table with his fingertip, keeping his gaze down. "Well, how I used to think of you, actually. Every time I got around you, just one look and I was like, I don't know, in heat or something."

Josh cleared his throat, desperate to know if he had any hope of reclaiming that affection and desire.

"And...now?" he asked, his voice husky as it ever got. "What do you think now, Hayden?"

Without any warning, Hayden's rich blue gaze lifted, locking with Josh's. Then, Hayden's black lashes lowered slightly, so that he stared up at Josh through them, an absolutely sensual expression on his face. "Isn't it obvious?" Hayden's lashes lowered a little more, creating the most utterly fuckable expression that Josh had ever seen on any person's face—male or female. "Wasn't it always obvious, that sexed-up reaction you got out of me?"

An absurd case of shyness swamped Josh in all of a second. He just sat there like some sort of mute, rubbing his neck and grinning like a fool. Well, and feeling his balls draw tight like they were winding up for a very fast pitch, with his hard-on offering itself as the required bat.

Finally, a semblance of Josh's mind returned, and he cleared his throat. "So, uh, let's talk about this elders' thing."

Hayden frowned back in silent reply; it was absolutely the most dumbass topic Josh could've possibly raised. But, despite his desire to drag Hayden back to his big ole bed, it was too soon to try something so blatant, and the truth was, Josh had to keep their process moving forward.

"Was it your idea?" Hayden asked him, point-blank.

When Josh didn't answer at first, Hayden scowled. "'Cause, I already told you, buddy, it wasn't mine."

"I'm well aware you didn't come up with the plan,"

Josh said, shifting his chair so he was facing Hayden better.

"So it was yours?" Hayden persisted.

Josh smiled sadly. "No, it really was all theirs," he admitted. "But I would have come for you in the next few months anyway."

Hayden cocked his head, clearly taken aback. "Why? I mean, after all this time, you were planning to look me up...or something?"

"Yes, in another eight months. That actually was my timetable." Josh flinched, thinking of the two men who had wanted to hurt his lover.

"I don't understand," Hayden answered, brushing long fingers through his hair with an absent gesture. "Eight months? It would have been almost six years since...I mean, what would have been the point, all this time later? We never even had much, Josh." Hayden leaned back in his chair, intelligent gaze trained on him, and Josh could practically see the man's keen mind shifting puzzle pieces, trying to see where this conversation was leading.

Hayden continued, voice intense. "Why were you even still thinking about me after all this time? Why would you have a plan—an actual timeframe—for coming to see me? We didn't have a real relationship, nothing."

Without meaning to, Josh balled his hands into fists right there on the table. "No choice...before," he managed to half-growl in reply. Slowly, Josh forced himself to relax his hands, to release the coiled fury that often overcame him when he remembered what had been done to Hayden.

"What were you thinking of just then?" Hayden asked, watching as Josh's fists flexed and relaxed and flexed again. "Why'd you get so upset? How did it relate to this timetable of yours?"

Josh's entire body grew taut, with him as on edge as he ever got in the thick of the hunt. Lowering his head in wolfish intent, he growled like the natural born predator he was. Hayden jerked back in his own chair, instinctively responding to the challenge of another Alpha.

Hayden's eyes flashed and then narrowed, his shoulders hunched forward, and he looked about ready to lunge when Josh released an anguished, soulful cry. "They wanted to hurt you. I couldn't let them do that. I-I didn't...couldn't." Josh felt the tears he'd kept inside for so many years tighten his throat, but he refused to cry in front of Hayden—especially when he considered how much more his lover had endured. "I did everything in my power, Hayden," he said finally, not daring to look into the other man's eyes. "To keep them from hurting you. From killing you, like they wanted to do."

Hayden was out of his chair and squatting beside Josh faster than any natural motion should have catapulted him. He reached for Josh's hand, seizing it with preternatural strength. He clutched it, staring up into Josh's anguished eyes. The ruined, broken look in them struck a chord, something familiar that Hayden couldn't recall, but which intensified the headache pounding behind his eyes.

"Joshua," he said, keeping his voice as steady as he could, "tell me who wanted to hurt me. Tell me what you're talking about."

Josh shook his head slightly, staring glassy-eyed across the room. "It kills me that you don't remember." Then he glanced down at Hayden. "Would you believe that all these years, some part of me really thought you knew. That you understood why I stayed away." Josh's voice broke and he scrubbed a hand across his eyes. "I hoped that at least you might have remembered what happened between us."

Hayden felt the floor beneath him nearly sway. "Tell me what I don't remember."

Josh buried his face in trembling hands. "There's just too much," he argued. "Too much fucked up shit that came right after. I don't want you to know all of it."

Hayden stood and, moving behind Josh's chair, bent low, wrapping his arms about the other man like a healing web of protection. "I'm here now, and I need to know." When Josh remained quiet, Hayden could hardly bear the silence. "At least tell me what happened between us, then," he urged.

Josh slid warm fingers up the length of Hayden's forearms, stroking him with more tenderness than Hayden had ever imagined Josh felt for him. "Hasn't the timeline of the accident seemed off to you? Wrong somehow?"

"It's..." Hayden felt like he was trying to pierce a dark, murky haze. He'd been in a coma for six weeks after the wreck, and the time in the courtroom, all of it had been a fog for him, his mind not fully recovered—it never had healed like it should, or he wouldn't have a giant blank canvas staring him in the eyes.

Josh squeezed his arms, turning his strong jaw against Hayden's shoulder. "We went out for beers on the twenty-ninth of December, right? By the time we took our run, then shared that—" Josh hesitated, then continued in a quieter voice,"—that sweet kiss, it was the early hours of December thirtieth. When we climbed in the truck, it was already the middle of the night."

Hayden didn't understand. What was Josh trying to make him figure out? "What are you getting at, Joshua?"

Josh slipped out of his grasp and stood, facing him. "Think, Hayden. Your mind has blocked out the details, and because of my testimony at the trial, you're not seeing the truth here."

Hayden couldn't piece the fractured parts of his memory together into whatever puzzle Josh wanted him to see. If it were possible, he'd have figured out the dark, vacant bits years before.

Josh's expression became fierce. "We weren't drunk. We'd been on a run! When would we have had time to drink?"

Hayden turned, began pacing. "I'd always assumed...those beers were still in our systems."

Josh moved with him, his voice becoming more agitated. "At six a.m. in the morning, Hayden? That's when the accident was. Just after six a.m.!"

Hayden pressed hands against his temples, trying to ease the splitting pain in his head. "It had to have been those beers."

Josh got right up in his face, gripping his arms tight. "I know what time we got in the truck, and it's not the time I had to claim to the police. It was right after two a.m."

Hayden jerked out of Josh's hold on him. "Wait, that's...that's four hours before the accident."

"There are four hours missing from your memories, Hayden. That's what I'm trying to tell you." Josh stared up at him, his green-blue eyes darkening.

Hayden couldn't breathe. It was as if all the beliefs he'd constructed for himself, starting in the hospital and later in prison, were collapsing on him. Crushing him.

And then a white hot pulse of fury set him on fire. Rounding on Josh, he slammed a fist into his jaw as hard as he could, sending the cop reeling back against the wall. Hayden was on him, pinning him there. "Why the fuck would you have lied to the police, then? At the trial? How could you have lied about where we were, the timing of it all? I always knew something smelled rotten about that night..."

Hayden drew back a hand to deck Josh again, but Josh's forearm came up, preventing him. A tangy scent filled the room and he realized he'd drawn blood from Josh's nose. The metallic odor instantly sobered him. Slowly, Hayden began to release his rough hold on Josh, but still kept him pinned against the wall. And Josh wasn't resisting—he was letting Hayden do whatever he wanted to him, as if willing to accept any abuse, if that's what it took to reach a breakthrough. No Alpha ever responded to a physical or emotional threat so passively, yet Josh just stared at him, ready to take whatever he dished out. All of it—Josh's responses, his words—felt surreal and downright unnatural.

"Why aren't you fighting back, you fucker?" Hayden seethed, breath coming hard and fast, just like Josh's. Their gazes locked in a battle of wills, huffing chests pressed close. "Tell me the fucking truth, for God's sake. I deserve at least that much."

Josh's eyes slid shut and he became incredibly still, slumping against the wall. "All right, Hayden. You do deserve the full truth, you're right." Josh's eyes remained closed and he whispered, "We became lovers that night. Spent hours together, making love, falling in love."

Hayden couldn't breathe, couldn't think. Felt as if the entire room was closing in on him, and his wolf side begged to break away.

"No...I would remember." He pressed his forehead against Joshua's, panting. "I know I'd remember."

Slowly Josh's eyes opened and a wistful, heartbroken smile formed on his face. "I'd never been with a guy before," he said, touching Hayden's cheek. "You were my first...my only. And I gave myself to you completely. Because I fell in love with you then. And I've never stopped loving you, not once in all these years."

Hayden took a step backward. Some quiet part of his

soul would know, would have to know. "No...you've got to be lying. Nothing would have driven us apart," he insisted. "Nothing could have."

Josh hardly seemed to hear him. "We drank shots of whiskey because I was nervous and you wanted me to relax. Because...well...so it wouldn't hurt." A deep flush filled Josh's face. "I guess we did get a little drunk, not too much. But it didn't hurt, you were right. You were so gentle with me, and I'd never felt anything like it before. No one had ever been so tender, so arousing. It was like you led me right to the stars and back, the way you touched me...everywhere. You set my body on fire and I fell so hard. Took no time at all." Josh met Hayden's shocked gaze, lifting a hand to slowly stroke Hayden's cheek. "Things...changed between us then."

Hayden couldn't fight the rush of rage, heartache— the insane swell of emotions warring in his head. He ducked sideways, escaping Josh's tender touch. "Things changed." Hayden growled. "Changed so much that I killed a man a few hours later."

Josh closed his eyes again, dropping his hand from Hayden's cheek. "Of course you didn't. It was all part of how our beautiful night came crashing down. You never broke any law, Hayden."

"I knew it," Hayden said, feeling absurdly triumphant, almost cruel, even as sharp tears burned his eyes. "I knew you set me up."

"Not me, Hayden." Josh shook his head with almost violent force. "I would have been willing to lie down in the road and die for you that night. For you, I'd have taken any bullet, any punishment." Josh laughed harshly. "And I guess, in a way, I did...I lost you. And I watched your life fall apart because of my choices."

Hayden couldn't take another moment of the deceit, the half-truths, the veiled intimations. Seizing Josh by the shoulders, he squeezed him hard and shook his entire body. "Tell me all of it, you fucker."

Josh's distant, pained gaze bore into Hayden. "All right. You want to know, I'll give it all to you. Then you can decide how you feel about the elders' proposition. About us mating."

"Won't happen," Hayden barked, keeping Josh pinned against the wall, wanting to throttle him, hold him, a thousand other things. "Never going to happen. You won't have that part of me."

"But that's just it, baby." Josh smiled again, his eyes lighting for the first time in the past few minutes. And then he began laughing, a lost, quiet sound. "I already do."

Hayden shook his head, the room almost spinning.

Josh leaned forward, pressing his lips against Hayden's mouth. "It's not day two of anything," he whispered gently. "There's no countdown to a decision, no need for us to fulfill the elders' mandate."

"Of course there is." Hayden shook his head, not following Josh's lost, dreamy-sounding words. "The council gave us thirty days," he said stupidly, hoping to keep the conversation on track.

"They can't give us a time limit to decide about

something that already exists," Josh told him softly. "They can't urge us to do what's already been done."

Hayden's heart nearly stopped in his chest, his mouth went dry. Was Joshua saying what he thought? "Wh-what do you mean?"

"We're already mated. It happened that night, when we made love for the very first time. So, you see..." Josh laughed wistfully, wiping at his eyes, "...there's a lot you don't recall. Including the fact that I belong to you, and you to me, Hayden, like it or not, for the rest of our lives."

Hayden's arms fell limp at his sides, and he felt as if his entire universe was unzipping, but Josh kept talking, saying things that Hayden couldn't even hear. Josh reached for him, tried to hold on, but Hayden's resistance was too strong.

Hayden couldn't stay, couldn't listen. He had to run, had to move into the darkening woods and turn feral. There was no escaping the pain, no way out, no way through what Josh was saying they'd lost.

With a savage growl, he sprang from the house and never looked back.

Chapter Eight

Five years earlier, December 30th, early a.m.

Hayden followed Josh into the other wolf's modest home, wildly curious as to what he might learn about his long-time obsession. Would the guy be a neat freak, a collector of bizarre knickknacks, a diehard gamer? Hayden had no idea what to expect and was subtly searching the place for any clues, his gaze sweeping the neat little kitchen with keen curiosity when Josh busted him.

"Yeah, it's not much," Josh said a tad defensively as he followed Hayden's inspecting glance. Then he shrugged. "But at least it's mine. Well, mine and the bank's." He laughed, tugging on his wool ski cap self-consciously, pulling it down over his ears.

"I think it's great." Hayden smiled his approval as he wandered all the way into the kitchen. "Besides, you don't see me owning my own digs yet. Pretty impressive at our age. And you've got lots of privacy out here."

They both fell silent at that comment, the reminder that they might really need some privacy for what they'd come here to do. Joshua stared at the floor, scuffing a snow boot wordlessly, and Hayden wasn't sure how the hell he was supposed to get the other Alpha into the bedroom at this point. Beneath the bright lights of the kitchen, the two of them had reclaimed their customary roles together, so it seemed downright unlikely. Especially with the way Joshua kept averting his eyes, appearing awkward and unsure about the whole situation. Why hadn't they just figured out how to blow each other in the damned truck? Maybe now things wouldn't be back to square zero.

Hayden sighed and took a step closer to Josh. "Look, dude," he began. "We don't have to... You know, maybe we just got a little carried away earlier, and if you don't want this. Don't want to, well, you know." Hayden coughed, clearing his throat, wishing Josh would pipe up and help him out, not leave him twisting in the proverbial wind. Instead, the guy just folded both arms over his chest, and looked toward the other side of the kitchen, toying with the zipper on his ski jacket.

Hayden raked a hand through his hair and tried again. "My point," he said in a tight, embarrassed voice, "is that maybe I should just head on home. If you don't want...this."

Josh began to smile then, giving him the blasted, cocky grin Hayden always found so annoying. The same one he'd flashed at the airport. His knowing smile indicated that Josh knew exactly how much Hayden lusted after him, how he craved and yearned so pointlessly. Joshua never looked up, but, oh yeah, he most definitely smirked.

"I'm gonna take off," Hayden blurted, feeling heat crawl from his neck all the way to his cheekbones. Had the other wolf been playing him the whole time? Just having a laugh, seeing exactly how far Hayden would try to go in an effort to get between his legs?

The sideways grin grew a little wider and for the first time Hayden noticed deep splotches of color on Josh's own face—and the way his hand trembled as he fiddled with his jacket. A thought occurred to Hayden then, such a radical revelation that he started smiling himself. Maybe Joshua Peterson wasn't so self-assured after all. And maybe he wasn't making fun of Hayden, nor getting his rocks off at how much Hayden longed for him.

Hayden's mind riffled through fractured bits of evidence, and suddenly he became convinced of one clear fact. All Josh's thrusting and touching back in the truck hadn't been a put on, nor had it been mockery. It had been the most passionate damned few moments Hayden had ever spent in any person's arms. And it had been real, as full of heat on Josh's side as on Hayden's.

Hayden pushed his wireframes up the bridge of his nose, suddenly confident again. "So, to quote the song, 'should I stay or should I go now'?"

"Good one, man." Josh laughed huskily. "I definitely don't want you to go. I'm just not sure what to do now that I've got you here, that's all," Josh admitted, his eyes lifting cautiously until that luminous green-gold gaze pinned Hayden hard. Speared him through the chest, the very soul. "I want you, though, Garrett. Promise you that. I'm just a little clueless. And...well, nervous as shit, frankly."

Hayden couldn't help it; he beamed. Josh wanted him and badly.

With his admission on the table, Josh's sideways grin spread a little wider, and he went back to tugging on his jacket zipper.

"Nervous as shit, huh?" Hayden repeated with a laugh.

"Uh...yeah. And horny as hell, too." Josh stared at the floor, still smiling.

Suddenly Hayden understood what had never become clear until that exact moment. Joshua's odd little smile wasn't smug or cocksure, not even close. All these years and Hayden had been reading the guy totally wrong.

Damn. Joshua Peterson was shy. Incredibly shy.

Hayden couldn't help it, but he began to laugh and Josh's eyes narrowed. "You're laughing at me?" The blush in his cheeks deepened to true crimson.

"Oh, no, baby. I'm laughing at me." He moved straight to where Josh leaned against the counter and cupped him beneath the chin. "Just never saw it coming."

Josh tilted his head sideways, a wolf's expression of quizzical confusion. "Saw...what coming?"

Hayden bent down, brushing his lips against Josh's with a very soft kiss. Tangling his fingers through the guy's unruly, damp hair, he murmured, "This shy streak of yours, Joshua, it's sexy as hell."

Josh growled, wrapping his arms about Hayden's

neck and deepening their kiss greedily. Then after a breath-stealing moment, one where their tongues warred and twined, where Hayden pushed his hips flush up against Josh's until their groins pressed together hard, Josh broke the kiss. Looking up into Hayden's eyes, he murmured, "I'm not that shy."

Hayden grinned in satisfaction. You never threw down a gauntlet to an Alpha wolf. Not if you didn't want very decisive results.

Josh was shaking all on the inside, and it was all he could do to keep those tremors from moving to the outside.

Garrett had him up against the counter, hands winding all through Josh's long, waving hair, hard body pinning him in place. But Josh, much as he wanted every damned touch of Garrett's, just couldn't stop shaking.

Hayden obviously picked up on those feelings because he hesitated, breaking their kiss. "What we need," Hayden offered in a knowing, gentle tone, "is some booze. To take the edge off."

Josh splayed his palms against Hayden's chest. "I've got whiskey."

"That'll do."

"I'm not a freak, man," Josh said, feeling embarrassed that he'd been hit with such a bout of nerves. "It's just my—"

Hayden stroked a thumb across Josh's lower lip, finishing the statement. "Your first time with another man."

"I've been with women. Just so you know." Josh tilted his head up proudly, defiantly. "I'm not inexperienced in bed."

"Still, for tonight, Joshua?" Hayden backed away, opening a cabinet, already looking for the liquor. "Tonight you're a virgin. My virgin."

Josh turned and retrieved two very large shot glasses, and pulled down a big bottle of whiskey. He had a feeling he was going to need it.

Hayden followed Josh down a small hallway, both men silent. Yet electric expectation seemed to crackle in the quiet atmosphere between them. When Josh reached the first doorway, he nudged open the door with his booted foot and stepped back with a gesture of playful gallantry.

"After you, Garrett." He didn't look up or meet Hayden's eyes, but swept a hand toward the room's interior. "My digs."

"The sacred chamber," Hayden said, slowly entering the room. And how long have I dreamed of getting in here. A fluttering sensation swept through the center of his belly. It was no time to get nervous, not tonight. Not when it was Joshua's first time.

The bedroom was plainly decorated and neat as any military officer's might be, as if awaiting inspection. The tidiness of the small room didn't shock him, but the walls of the space sure did. There were floor to ceiling bookshelves lined with a diverse selection of novels and books. He'd always known Josh was smart—he'd learned that much firsthand in high school—but somehow Hayden figured the other wolf wouldn't have much to do with books.

"You like to read," Hayden observed and it wasn't a question. "No, let me correct that. I think you love to read."

"So do you."

Hayden walked to the first bookshelf, running his fingertips along the row of volumes, fascinated to see how closely their tastes intersected. "You have always surprised the hell out of me, Joshua."

"Like tonight?" Josh's question was throaty, full of sexual intensity.

Hayden swallowed, keeping his back to the other Alpha. Damn if he wasn't the one who'd begun shaking, quite literally, in his snow boots.

"Especially tonight," he agreed, struggling to rein in his physical reaction.

He heard the bedroom door close, and turned to find Josh leaning against it, both hands pressed behind his lower back. He stood there with an air of finality and resolve, all his earlier nervousness gone. Yet his face was even more flushed than it had been in the kitchen, red blotches high on his defined, sculpted cheekbones.

Josh had deposited the whiskey bottle and pair of shot glasses on his wooden bureau, and as Hayden stared at the dresser, he thought about Josh keeping his clothes inside the damned thing. Instantly he recalled the man's fresh, earthy smell, how it was like the woods after a spring rain. Hayden was certain the flannel shirts, and jeans, and long underwear Josh kept in his bureau would carry the same delicious scent.

Josh pushed off the door, and removed his stocking cap, tossing it onto the center of the bed as if it were a choice prize. As if were marking the bed as the prime circus ring...no, as if they were about to box or wrestle and that simple wool hat was the physical invitation.

The front of Hayden's pants drew tight, instantly uncomfortable and too constricting as his mind provided a visual of Joshua's naked, sculpted body in the center of the bed, not his cap. Of diving forward for the true prize, the man who he'd secretly loved and desired for years now.

Neither spoke, but Josh moved to sit on the edge of the bed, removing first one boot, then the other. As if he meant to do nothing so much as get truly down to business. Now it was Hayden who stood, a little paralyzed by the moment, watching Josh from the side of the room. Hayden had to swallow hard as he noticed that Josh's hair was still damp from their tussle in the snow. Or perhaps it was wet from how sweaty they'd gotten while making out in the truck? Either way, Hayden grew even harder realizing it was his touch, his kisses that had caused Josh to become so disheveled.

The memory of how incredibly intimate they'd gotten quashed his own bout of nerves and he moved toward the bed decisively, stripping out of his sweatshirt as he went.

Josh glanced up, eyes widening first, then growing bright, otherworldly. And Hayden was absolutely transfixed by the beauty of those golden-green irises, the flecks of light blue and amber—and the way Josh dropped his long black lashes low as he studied Hayden's bare chest.

Keeping his gaze pinned on Hayden and licking his lips wolfishly, Josh slowly removed his own shirt, stripping his chest bare. He eased back on the bed, propping his back against the headboard. Hayden had never seen a more developed physique—and he had glimpsed Josh shirtless plenty of times back in high school when they'd played on the same baseball and football teams. But Josh had filled out tremendously since then, especially in the past year, and now possessed cordons of muscle that knotted across his flat abdomen, as well as powerful biceps and shoulders. Josh wasn't tall compared to him, but he was strong and bulky through the upper body. Hayden let his gaze travel lower, to Josh's jean-clad lower body, and instantly recalled the feeling of the man's strong thighs about his hips. The truck with Josh had been glorious. But being in the bed with him, naked? Was going to be downright rapturous.

Josh caught Hayden ogling him. "Like what you see, do you, Alpha?" he teased, leaning back a little farther so that his sculpted chest stood out even more sexily. Josh stroked lazy fingers across his abdomen, lingering at the waistband of his jeans with a suggestive look. No more shy guy. Interesting.

"I've always liked the look of you, baby," Hayden returned, chucking his sweatshirt onto the floor. "You've always known it, too. My soul be damned, but I could never hide my feelings from you...or hide how you aroused me."

"Your scent always shocked me. I never knew what the hell to do about it—or about you, Hayden. But I do now." With an unabashedly wicked grin, Josh patted the place beside him on the mattress. "Come on, Alpha. Bring the whiskey." Then Josh growled, low and sexy right in the very back of his throat. "And drop the jeans while you're at it."

They rolled to face each other, the bed giving a creaking groan. It was a weathered four-poster, hardly quiet for lovemaking. Good thing Josh's house sat way off the road without a neighbor nearby, what with all the ruckus his old bed was going to make. Being silent or even quiet wasn't going to be possible, not while making love to Josh.

Hayden slid a hand down to Josh's hip, took hold and urged him a little closer. Josh ran his tongue over his own lips and complied. The guy began trembling as their groins brushed together, even though they still wore jeans. Was it with fear? Arousal? Hayden wasn't sure, but the hair on his nape bristled when he caught the faint aroma of Josh's mating scent.

"You need another shot of whiskey," Hayden told him softly and sitting up in bed, reached for the bottle. The bed groaned again and Hayden laughed. "Does the bed make always make this much noise...when you bring females here?"

"Wouldn't know." Josh poured himself a shot and tossed it back.

"Thought you were Mr. Experienced." Hayden couldn't help being curious. If Josh was so big with the ladies, then why hadn't he ever brought any of them home?

Josh met his surprised stare and smiled. "Never asked anyone back to my place before now, that's all," he admitted, color hitting his cheeks again.

Hayden leaned forward and kissed him, chest tight as a drum. *I'm the first he's ever trusted like this.*

Pulling back, Hayden gazed long and hard into the other wolf's magnetic eyes. They'd changed color again, those flecks of amber far more pronounced than usual.

Sliding his hand back to Josh's hip, he rubbed him there, then slowly slid his palm between the man's thighs, palming his groin. A thick ridge bulged through the center of Josh's jeans, punching the zipper out, and protruding boldly. Hayden took his fingertips and very gently traced the outline of the other wolf's erection. He'd have sworn it bulged even more beneath his hand.

"I like this," Hayden growled in a throaty voice. "A lot." He allowed his touch to grow firmer, become an actual stroking caress as he traced Joshua's thick hard-on once again.

Hayden's hand paused at the zipper, and he ran his fingers along the length of it, feeling the way the metal bowed outward with Josh's erection. Josh jolted slightly in reaction, reaching toward Hayden. With a moan, he sank his fingers into Hayden's hair, arching slightly.

Hayden whispered against Josh's sandpapery cheek, "I know firsthand that you are neither a boxer nor a briefs man, so I'm going to be very gentle about this." Hayden popped the button of Josh's jeans and with infinite slowness eased the zipper down. Josh truly began trembling in earnest then, right as Hayden peeled back those jeans and Josh's cock sprang free from the fabric's confines.

With his right hand, Hayden gripped the blunt head of Josh's thick erection. With his left, he moved inside Josh's open pants, sliding his palm behind until his fingertips found the man's muscular buttocks. Kissing Joshua, Hayden moved his hand behind and underneath him until he found the man's sweet spot of arousal. Working his fingertips at the puckered opening, Hayden gave him a gentle, exploratory stroke.

Josh bucked and inhaled harshly in reaction, obviously shocked when Hayden's fingertips probed his sensitive spot. Can't push too fast, Hayden cautioned himself and slid that hand up to the base of Josh's spine, stroking him soothingly. He'd wait to touch Josh's private place again, allow the other Alpha to relax into his arms a bit more—and reach a more fevered level of need.

Hayden focused his full attention on Josh's cock, rubbing his thumb forcefully over the slit until warm dampness formed beneath his fingertips. Until Josh buried his face against Hayden's shoulder with a loud, uninhibited moan of pleasure.

Hayden stroked harder, the wetness in his palm growing, and he spread it in a teasing circle around the tip of Josh's erection. Then back to the head for more wet slickness, which he used to work his way in an aggressive rhythm down to the thick base of Josh's cock. He then took hold of the man's twin sacs, pleasuring him until Josh's hips rode of the mattress, rolling on a stroke of Hayden's hand.

"That's it, Joshua. Give in to me."

He wanted to arouse Josh, tantalize him—fulfill his needs so thoroughly that he would never want a woman, not ever again. Make him so caught in Hayden's own thrall that Josh would follow him to the very ends of the earth to hold him once more.

At that precise moment, the mating scent erupted powerfully all across Josh's body, the aroma so rich, Hayden swore he might get drunk off it.

Josh was desperate to get his hand on Hayden Garrett's cock. There was only one problem with that plan: Josh was terrified to reach across the few inches separating his groin from Hayden's. It was a ridiculous form of paralysis, considering Hayden was slicking a palm low and hard down Josh's own hard-on. As Hayden's strokes grew more aggressive, Josh moaned...again. He'd been unable to stop moaning, in fact, and the rising fever of need and desire only made him ache to touch Hayden even more.

With eyes pressed closed, Josh reached toward the firm length that kept bumping into his own thigh, and with a thrilling gasp, felt warm skin brush into his palm.

He dared to look then, gazing down to see that Hayden's boxers had slipped open, his hard, warm flesh protruding invitingly. He rubbed a tentative thumb over the crown, imitating the way Hayden had initially touched Josh, then with a firm, long stroke—knowing what felt so damned pleasurable to him—he began stimulating the man. What he got as a reward was a thing of sheer beauty.

Hayden moved onto his back, tugging the cotton boxers low down his hips and began moving with Josh's hard caresses, all the while keeping up his own gentle friction on Josh's arousal. Then Hayden rolled to face him again, much closer this time. So close, Josh could feel the other wolf's heated, panting breath against his jaw—so close that as their hands tightened in a grip about the other's erections, moving faster and faster, their knuckles bumped. Their fingers grazed. Their sweat mingled between their thighs and groins.

Hayden shocked him by reaching mid-motion, and twining a pinkie with Josh's, never stopping his fluid, arousing force on Josh's cock. Their hands began moving almost as one, creating divine pleasure unlike any Josh had never known in his life.

He felt his erection pulse, the veins tightening, and he pressed a staying hand against Josh's knuckles. "Garrett," he warned. "I'm going to lose it totally if you keep this up."

Hayden leaned his jaw against Josh's, brushing his cheek back and forth against the bristle of Josh's goatee as if savoring it. "If you lose it, my virgin, it's only going to be to me tonight. But if you come in my hand, I'll just get you hard all over again."

Josh quivered at the words, the seductive promise, and lifted a thigh up around Hayden's right hip. With a familiar slide—familiar yet utterly brand new—he slid his straining cock between Hayden's legs. Instead of that hidden wetness he was accustomed to with a woman, he reveled in the hard warmth of gliding against Hayden's own hardness. Gasped at the pressure of their twin erections pushing and warring in a back and forth pressure—at the velvet hardness of the sensations, contrasted with the much softer press of Hayden's sacs.

"Why did we wait this long?" Josh blurted without being able to stop the words. "All the time..."

Hayden groaned in his ear. "You didn't want me."

"I did." Because Josh suddenly knew he had wanted Hayden Garrett, ever since their first run together several years earlier. "I always wanted you. I just didn't understand."

"I've loved you for years, Joshua."

Josh pressed his eyes shut, trembling all over, aching to feel the pressure of Hayden deep within him. "Take me, Alpha. Now. Right now."

Thank God Josh was into self-pleasuring and did it in style. Otherwise, he never would have had what they desperately needed for this first time, and it wasn't like the drug store was open at two a.m.

Josh fumbled with the bedside drawer and tossed a small tube to Hayden, flushing like he'd just spent the day over on the slopes of Snow King.

Hayden smiled, was fast about his task, then bent low between Josh's legs, gently working the slippery stuff against his tender opening. "We've had plenty of whiskey, baby, and I'm gonna be gentle. Just like I promised. Still," Hayden warned, "you've got to relax. You're tensed up back here."

Josh nodded, sinking back into the pillow obediently, urging his hips upward so Hayden could get a better position as very slowly, very tenderly, he slid a single finger into Josh's tight opening. Josh yelped loudly at that first erotic probing.

"Fuck," he blurted under his breath.

Hayden leaned down and kissed him slowly on the belly, wanting to ease his fear and tight emotions. "True. That's exactly the idea."

"Shut up, college boy," Josh muttered with a low laugh. At that exact moment, Hayden slid a second finger inside, spreading Josh a little, taking advantage of the humorous, relaxed moment to get him wider.

Once he'd worked at the opening, preparing his lover, he levered his hips upward until he was positioned atop Josh perfectly. He heard the other Alpha suck in a sharp, expectant breath—as if he were waiting to be slugged across the jaw.

"I know this is going to hurt like hell," Josh murmured, eyes pressed tight in wincing anticipation.

"I'm going to turn pain into the sweetest pleasure you've ever known," Hayden promised, pushing at the man's taut opening. No give at all. He put more force into the motion and gained a good inch, and this elicited a long, low moan from Josh.

Hayden kissed him encouragingly. "That's it," he promised. "I'm going slow, baby. Really slow."

He gained more purchase, easing and forcing his way into his lover, an inch or so at a time. When he'd managed to sheath himself about halfway, Josh suddenly clutched at Hayden's shoulders, grinding harsh fingers into the muscles. "Garrett, this burns like hell," Josh gasped. "It...I don't know. I'm...it's like you're setting me on fire. Fucking hell. I just don't know if I can—"

Hayden silenced the frantic protest with a full-mouthed kiss, promising the world to this man whom he'd forever craved—all with the stroke of his own tongue. "It's okay, Joshua," he murmured, finally breaking the kiss. "It's okay. It'll get better soon...feel better. You're just a virgin, that's all."

"Not...really." Josh grunted uncomfortably, his expression tight.

"Anyone ever come inside of you before?" Hayden whispered against his lover's jaw, loving the tickle of Josh's goatee against his own smooth skin. "Any man ever get between your legs like this, Joshua?"

"You're...it. You know that." Josh dug his fingers into Hayden's back. "But God, you're big..."

"So you're a virgin, baby. Totally mine. And you know what they say about losing your virginity, right?"

Josh shook his head and groaned as Hayden pushed

in a great deal deeper, desperate to get his lover's pain over with. "No. Tell...me."

Hayden moved his hips with the strongest force yet at that precise second. "A moment of pain, a lifetime of bliss." And with his firm motion, he felt Josh's whole body react, those gorgeous eyes flipping open.

"Holy mother!" Josh barked, hands and arms wrapping all about Hayden in desperation. "Oh, yeah, Garrett. Yeah!"

Hayden grinned and began showering the other wolf with gentle, probing kisses. He'd just reached the man's most sensitive, erogenous spot. Now Joshua Peterson understood exactly what Hayden could offer him, how he could love him. And he'd realized that no woman would ever be able to do for him—to him—what Hayden could.

Their bodies were a perfectly choreographed, sluicing movement of one. The deeper and harder Hayden rode Josh, the more the other man reacted—crying out, moaning, howling. The sounds alone were enough to get Hayden off, they were so sensual and reactive. He'd never had a lover as expressive as Josh before, and as they drove their hips together, crashing like waves of electric desire, a strange thought passed through Hayden's mind: Joshua intended to take him as mate. Somehow Hayden knew this was far more than lovemaking. It was ownership.

The thought carried a thrilling accompanying scent.

Joshua, head thrown back, a look of utter ecstasy on

his face, was marking him as his mate. The scent was slowly seeping between them, layering over Hayden's own body like possessive cologne, like a mate's musk.

Panicking at the realization, he stilled inside Josh. Not that Hayden wouldn't thrill to have him for a mate, but they were just now coming together for the first time. Surely the other Alpha didn't intend…

Josh's eyes opened and he lifted his head off the pillow. "Why'd you stop?" The tone was nearly like begging, his hands already reaching to urge Hayden back into a stroking rhythm.

Hayden leaned down, brushing damp, waving locks of hair away from Josh's eyes with both hands. For a moment, he said nothing. Then whispered, "You're marking me."

Josh's eyes drifted shut, and he sank back into the pillow. "Oh…yeah."

"Joshua," Hayden murmured more firmly. "You can't. You really shouldn't mark me."

"Why not?" Josh asked languidly, eyes still closed, hands roving across Hayden's lower back, sliding lower still.

Hayden gripped Josh's chin. "Because it can't be undone, baby. You know that."

"I thought you wanted me," he said in a slightly dazed tone, and suddenly Hayden wondered if Josh had gotten drunker off the whiskey than he'd realized. "You said you wanted me," Josh repeated, finally opening his eyes again. They were pure darkness, the amber that usually lurked in the irises gone.

"Look, Josh, you know I do, but mating is for life."

All at once, Josh leaned up on his elbows, incredibly lucid, his musky marking scent flowering even more potently between them. The fragrance was heavy, possessive. "If you don't want to mate," he told Hayden plainly, "you'd better get off of me and leave the house, because I can't stop this. It's beyond my control."

Hayden gaped down at him, slowly moving his hips again despite himself. "Your marking me is...you can't control...what?"

Josh collapsed back into the pillows, tightening his thighs about Hayden's hips. "You're my mate, Garrett. I knew it the minute you got all the way inside me. Instinct's taken over," he said, groaning slightly. "So if you don't want me, then get the fuck away. Otherwise, take me. Now."

Hayden felt tears burn his eyes as a freight train of an orgasm shot to his groin. "I claim you," he cried in reply. "Mate, you are mine."

With those words, his own marking scent flowed out of his pores, rolled out of him in waves just as he felt his orgasm erupt. For long slow moments, they panted, Josh's own cock equally spent, their bodies burning and slick.

That was when the next mating wave hit them both with the primal force of nature.

Ungrounded lightning pulsed between them, a

physical bond that spun like an iron spider web, uniting them. Electrifying them. Growing hard, solid. Tangible. Hayden gasped in reaction, gulping at air. His eyes watered and his entire body jackknifed as their mating union formed. He could feel it, in the core of his heart and soul, a connection so vital, he knew nothing could ever shatter it. They would never be cut apart, never divided, not after this moment of pure union. For weeks, this bond would deepen, grow stronger, richer. They'd not even be able to transform to their wolf bodies, the supernatural process was that intense.

As the sensations gained strength, began pummeling through Hayden's shoulders, his chest, he sensed and felt Joshua Peterson as if he existed within his own soul. He knew his mate's mind and thoughts, felt the beating tempo of the other wolf's heart, the same as if it pounded within his own chest. The mating act was complete. They were fully one, connected together by a link so permanent, no man or wolf could ever sever it. United by a tether forged of steel, one only death itself would ever manage to dissolve.

The avalanche of physical and emotional sensations reached a shaking crescendo. The spiritual joining crested, climaxing, and as it did so, their bodies sang in response. Hayden felt Josh's cock thicken into a hard wedge, pushing sharply between them. Hayden's own erection hardened all over again, pushing deep within Josh. Lengthening, throbbing until the mating peace he'd felt moments before transformed. Instantly, that thrilling stillness was replaced by something much more primitive and animalistic. His wolf nature awakened, although he remained in human form. Thrusting his head back, Hayden released a long, singing howl.

Josh wrapped both arms about Hayden, clinging as if his life depended upon it, and answered Hayden's cry with a wild call of his own. Back and forth they sang, growing more erect, more aroused, until desire rolled through Hayden like a pure explosion of need.

"Oh, God, baby!" Hayden barked on a string of sputtering curses. His body was a shaking, rutting mess, and he was so out of control, he feared he might come in less than five seconds. "Joshua! Damn." He began thrusting with ferocious intent, blind to anything but the pure wolf instinct now in charge. His balls drew tight, pulling harshly, and he knew he was going to come almost as quickly as he'd hardened. Josh clearly experienced the same climax—and at the same precise moment—because his erection jerked between their bellies, spasming with orgasm. Josh groaned, arching back into the pillow, his hips riding hard off the mattress.

"Hayden!" he cried out, digging his fingers into Hayden's buttocks, moving in union with Hayden's frantic, demanding surges. Each time, Josh rose up, meeting the thrusts, spurting warm, coating jets between their bellies and chests.

Hayden finished off like a rocket himself, finally shouting and howling his release. Then they were rolling together, frenzied and not even close to true mating completion. Hayden had the dim thought that this ancient binding, this truly animalistic side of theirs, wasn't nearly satisfied yet. They tumbled first in one direction and then the other until Josh was straddled atop him, spreading his own ejaculation between Hayden's legs, coating him with a desperately shaking hand. With one quick glance, Hayden saw that his mate had grown erect a third time, the gleaming length of his arousal bobbing outward as he slicked Hayden for sex.

"I need to be inside of you," Josh explained, panting in short bursts. "If I don't fucking get inside you right now, I'm gonna fucking explode. I'm gonna come all over your belly if I can't just get inside you. Right now."

Hayden understood the sentiment and spread his legs eagerly, falling under Josh's suddenly very commanding sway. He didn't mind feeling Beta, not if his Alpha turned him on this powerfully. He wasn't fully erect again, although his own arousal was starting to thicken and stretch anew. Damn, it was a level of physicality he'd never experienced before, not by himself, and certainly not with any other man he'd ever slept with. It had to be the mating act, had to be the marking scent all over their naked bodies.

Josh knelt between Hayden's legs, still spreading slickness in preparation, and Hayden reached with a fumbling hand toward the bedside table. He grabbed the lube, giving it to Josh. "You'll still need more of this."

With a curse, Josh took the stuff, mumbling in frustration. "I don't know what the hell I'm doing. Man, I'm sorry, I'm a mess. I don't have a fucking clue what's right or wrong. I just know what I want. Who I want." Josh lifted his bright gaze, locking on Hayden like a laser.

"I know if I don't take you in about thirty seconds, Garrett, I'm gonna explode or something. This mating urge is making me...horny as fucking hell!" Josh started laughing, brushing a damp lock of hair away from his eyes as he kept slicking Hayden's opening, preparing him with shaking hands.

Hayden leaned up off the mattress until he faced Josh, and he took his mate's face between both palms, hoping to still his manic reaction to their full mating. "Joshua," he said firmly, but the other Alpha only planted slick palms on both of Hayden's thighs, staring downward.

Hayden dragged Josh's mouth to his. "Joshua, look at me," he demanded, and slowly Josh's gaze lifted until their eyes met across the short distance. "You are everything I ever wanted in all my life. This night? It's my dream. You were always my dream. You're my mate. How can you disappoint me?"

Josh leaned forward, pressing their foreheads together, still trembling all over. "I don't understand what's happening. The way my body's reacting to this mating, it's too much. It's like, if I can't just get this—" he reached between them, tugging on his erection," —inside you, and now, I'm going to die. Or shatter...or..." Josh shook his head, and Hayden slid a hand to his nape, pinning him close.

"Breathe, babe. I already belong to you. It's your wolf's mating instinct, but you can breathe. You claimed me. I'm yours now. I'm already yours. Just slow down a little, okay. Relax and hold onto me."

"You're mine," Josh repeated on a deep exhale. "Mine."

Hayden nodded slowly, covering Josh's mouth slowly, dragging his lower lip between his teeth. He sank his tongue deep into Josh's mouth then, and in a flurry of arms and limbs, they rolled down onto the mattress. Their hands were all in each others' hair. Hayden's legs were opening wide, and with a mystical grace, he felt Josh pushing into the edge of his opening.

Hayden nodded his approval, thrusting his tongue deep within the other man's warm cavern of a mouth. Josh's marking scent began to flow off his skin anew, covering Hayden like the sweetest, most arousing dew. Like nectar from a rare, exotic plant, it filled his nostrils, stimulating him, and he answered in kind, marking Joshua's entire body as his mate pushed farther and farther inside.

This was what forever felt like. It had to be.

Chapter Nine

Present day

The full moon rose in the distant sky, appearing unusually large. Hayden lifted his head high, sniffed at the air with his wolf's senses, and released a mournful, plaintive cry. It had been days since he'd left Joshua chasing after him as he tried to make sense of the man's surreal words. Every time Hayden recalled them, he was swamped with new grief, new confusion.

The council can't urge us to do what's already been done.

It wasn't just those words that haunted him, either, but the raw expression on Joshua's face, the broken, exhausted look in his vivid eyes. All of it chased Hayden more relentlessly than Josh had tried to do. The questions storming through his wolf's mind were endless, and he vacillated between believing Josh told the truth about their mating, and deciding the Alpha was spinning a complex web of lies.

For five years Hayden had been heartbroken, lost— and, as Joshua observed—falling apart. Convinced that the only person he had ever loved or yearned for had turned on him as a traitor.

Surely he would remember making love with Joshua, mating with him for life. Wouldn't he? How could he forget something so intense, so utterly primal that it came from their deepest wolf's nature—and especially if the mating had happened with Joshua of all men.

Except, of course, he recalled nothing after their sweet, spellbinding kiss in the snow. Everything was a blank canvas from that point onward. Right up until the moment when he emerged from his six-week long coma. Right up until the cops had arrived at the intensive care ward, questioning him about the accident—an accident he couldn't recall in the slightest.

Staring at the moon, Hayden forced his mind back to that night, determined to seize hold of at least a single fractured memory. Something to validate or disprove what Joshua had claimed about their relationship.

Perhaps it was the moon's fullness or maybe the sheer intensity with which Hayden probed his lost memories, but an image flooded his mind suddenly. Flashing like a beacon into his consciousness, it startled him, rang with all the truth of genuine recollection— Joshua naked, straddling him in the truck, thrusting his hips hungrily.

Hayden grew stock still, and listened to the night sounds of the land about him, smelled the snow. The splintered image expanded, blossoming into a much fuller memory. He could taste Joshua's mouth, scent his intense arousal. A spicy aroma filled his nostrils, so rich and musky, it could easily have been wafting past his nose now—and it matched the scent he'd caught off of Joshua in the bar the other night. It was the Alpha's undeniable, alluring mating scent. The one Josh had claimed was meant to draw Hayden to his side, to compel him to mate.

Hayden sank down on his hind legs, then folded down onto the snowy earth, planting his head atop his paws. A deep, mournful emotion filled him, alarming his very soul. All at once he did remember. And he recalled Joshua's mating scent—not just from a few nights ago—but from long, long ago, as well. If only his memories would yield, giving him more details, more information. He released a plaintive, melancholy whine.

If Joshua had been telling the truth about their mating, then Hayden's reaction to the confession must have killed him. Must have nearly destroyed whatever was left of the man's heart. Might even have shattered whatever pitiful remnant remained of their original mating bond. Mates shared a psychic connection, a deep, pulsing link, which he and Josh didn't have, so perhaps their mating had never fully taken hold.

I have to remember more...have to confirm it all with my own mind and heart.

He wasn't sure how much remained in the elders' timeframe now. But he felt pretty certain he'd been roaming for at least seven days, which didn't leave him long to determine how he planned to respond to the council's proposal. Of course, if Josh was telling the truth, then the elders weren't even a factor in their mating equation. But the lack of psychic, soul-joining bond between them certainly would be. How could he and Joshua engage a connection that didn't live between them? Their bond would be the mating proof the council demanded in order to sanction a joining between their two rival clans. It would be the proverbial wedding night test, and the elders' were more than able to validate the link between any two mates—gay or not.

Hayden rose and bounded into the woods, determined that before he returned to Joshua, he'd reclaim the blank place in his memories. Then, and only then, would he return to the man he'd never stopped loving, ready to face their future, not their past.

"What happened to that totally cocky Alpha brother of mine?" Kira demanded, leaning both palms against the other side of his desk. She lowered her head, staring at him with eyes the same bright shade as Josh's own. "And to your big, macho plan about wooing your mate, proving your love to him once and for all? I guess all that talk was nothing but hot air, huh?"

"Sis, don't try and provoke me," Josh said miserably, glancing up at his closed office door to ensure they really did have privacy for this particular chat.

His younger sister wasn't about to be daunted—and such bold strength and tone were atypical for her, which only made his utter failure all the more depressing.

"Kira, I failed. Period." He shook his head sadly. "I haven't seen Hayden in eight days. He bounded away and turned wolf before we were even finished with the conversation, and I couldn't catch him. He was too fast, hurting too much...and he's still a stronger Alpha than me. Flat out, he outran me and never looked back."

He'd been certain Hayden would respond to him, to his touch, his love, his confessions. But he'd underestimated just how far gone his mate was—and the impact of his own choices, ones which had brought his lover to such a low state.

He buried his face in his hands, willing the heartache away—willing their pasts to somehow, magically, be different. If only Hayden had never left his bed and house that early morning, but had instead called his folks and just...stayed. If only they'd held each other till the sun came up, till the fire in their loins had cooled. God, they would have made love all the next day, deepening and strengthening their mating bond, if only Hayden hadn't driven away.

The "if onlys" were enough to make Joshua insane if he contemplated them long enough.

Kira moved around to his side of the desk, and, wrapping her lean arms about his neck, held him tight. "It's not over yet, Joshua. Don't you dare give up, not with as hard as you've fought to get here. You've made sure he's safe. Those creeps are behind bars...now you make Hayden see how much he means to you. You get him to understand the truth."

Josh hugged her and then rolled his chair backward, escaping her embrace. "I can't find him, or you know that I would."

She sat down on the edge of his desk, chewing her lower lip in thought. "So where do you think he is? On his own pack's land?"

"Probably."

"And you can't go there, obviously—but can you send someone after him? His father?"

"His mom and dad have searched for him repeatedly over the past week. Followed his tracks, his scent, but they vanish in the river. He's like a ghost wolf."

She sighed, clearly understanding his frustration and pain. "Well then, you wait for him to come to you. You dig in and get really patient for once. It's going to have to be on his terms. That's obviously the message he's trying to send you."

Josh lifted his head, experiencing his first real hope since Hayden had vanished. "You think this is some kind of statement? His running like this?"

She rolled her eyes, smiling at him like he was a true idiot. "Look, you've got to do something radical here. Something that doesn't come naturally to you, especially not with Hayden Garrett. You've got to stop blaming yourself so much. And you've also got to let go of your huge protective streak. Hard for an Alpha when his mate is in pain or threatened, I know."

Josh growled low, an unstoppable instinct, then fell silent so his sister could continue.

"Just this once, sweetie," she said, "you've got to allow this to go slow. Let your mate determine things...decide when he's ready. Because there's only one way you'll wind up with what you want."

"I don't understand. What do you think I should do?"

"Simple." She gave him a gentle, sympathetic smile. "You sit back and let Hayden Garrett come to you."

Hayden settled in his makeshift den, rolling onto his side in sleepy agitation. It was morning, and he'd run for hours the night before. Sleep was demanding its due, which suited Hayden since these half-awake moments always yielded the richest, most vivid of his missing memories.

Closing his eyes, he lulled himself into sleep the way he always did these days; by thinking of Joshua and reviewing images and clues from their past, a past Hayden was slowly piecing back together. Soon he would return to human form—and to the human world he'd fled several weeks earlier.

By his calculations, he'd been roaming for seventeen days, maybe a day or two longer, he couldn't be sure. He'd hunted and roved his pack's land, had felt more wild and feral than ever before in his life. But he'd also done something far more important: He'd reclaimed four hours of missing memories. Only one blank spot remained, and even that was beginning to fill in because of his intense scrutiny.

As the hazy darkness had parted, revealing the truth of his past, he'd relived each awakening memory as if for the first time. As if it was not from five years in the past, but instead as if it were happening now. Hayden shifted again on his side, feeling dozy—yet impatient. The sooner he filled in of the last piece of his memories, the sooner he could...well, he had a whole list of plans for what he'd do then, but that moment wasn't upon him just yet.

Sleep began to tug at him more strongly, and he once again relived the first time he and Josh had made love. God, it had been sweet, just like he'd promised it would be. Josh had a shockingly shy streak, and it had endeared him to Hayden even more, the way he'd grinned and tried to seem so unflappable. The bravado had crumbled almost immediately, however, with Josh leaning against his kitchen counter, shivering with arousal and nervousness. Then as they'd come together, Josh's Alpha streak had emerged full blaze, the two of them almost battling together in that bed. Battling, claiming, joining, their sweat-slick bodies sliding together as if they'd been created for only one purpose. For those long, rough, erotic strokes and thrusts they shared as they became fully one.

As sleep claimed Hayden, a new memory flashed through his mind. Such a sexy and sweet one, imbued with utter contentment. The moment had been at the end of their lovemaking, and his body had felt sated, a little sore. A warm buzz humming through every cell in his body, he'd hated to leave Josh, even though he had no choice. So he'd climbed out of Joshua's bed, prepared to head back to his folks house for a few hours. Long enough to shower and change, invent some reason why he would be gone most of the day, and then return to Josh.

As Hayden hurriedly dressed, sliding his wireframes on, Josh stretched his arms overhead with a lazy yawn, revealing thatches of dark, curling hair beneath both arms. It was such a sexy, masculine picture, Hayden's groin did a leaping two-step of excitement.

With a wicked grin, Joshua lowered a hooded, languorous gaze to the front of Hayden's jeans. "You know, I've got a new goal in life. Getting that reaction out of you, Garrett, and as often as possible. That is one hell of a gorgeous sight...you all worked up over me."

"Cut it out," Hayden said, finding his wireframe glasses on the side table. He slid them over his eyes, and Josh came into much clearer view, which only made him more irresistible. "I've got to hit the road, baby. You know that."

Josh folded his forearms beneath his head, still eyeing Hayden with a wolfish gleam in his exotic eyes. "Can't blame me for trying to seduce you. Good God, after what we just did together, Hay?" Josh lifted an arm, acting as if he were up at bat. "We'll call that the wind up. I'm only getting started with you. Home run yet to come."

Yet to come. Why did Josh's choice of words seem far from accidental?

Hayden flushed, imagining what Josh might have in mind. And already debating between climbing back atop him and going for said home plate all over again—or driving back to the house so his parents wouldn't worry. He hadn't brought his cell phone, and was afraid phoning them from Josh's home or cell might garner suspicion. Breaking the news of his chosen mate was going to require quite a bit of finesse, especially considering they were each the heir apparent to their respective—and

138

longtime rival—clans.

Josh was a model of determination. "Come on, man," he said forcefully. "One more go before you hit the road." Joshua studied him with a greedy, sensual expression. "It's cold outside, but my bed is all warmed up for you." He patted the rumpled sheets in invitation, just as he'd done a few hours before. "There's even a little whiskey left. Imagine how warm you'll feel with me between your legs again. Of course, there's always that snow-covered, frigid SUV of yours out there." Josh lazed backward, spreading his legs open, his rigid cock falling against his taut abdomen. He gave his erection a slow, sensual tug, never taking his gaze off Hayden. "Your choice, college boy."

Hayden's whole body tightened in lusty agreement, his jeans becoming like a vise about his groin. But a quick glance at his watch tamed his eager reaction, and had him pulling on his hiking boots. "It's almost five-thirty, baby," he said. "Got to get back to the folks, make up some excuses about where I'll be...and then get right back to you. They're gonna freak otherwise."

"Tell them you belong to me now."

"Shit, Joshua, they're gonna smell you all over me if I'm not careful, but we've got to break this news slow and easy. And you know why."

Josh had growled deep from his chest right then. "How long?" he asked in a frustrated tone. "'Cause just so you know, all I want right now is to have you to myself. All day long, you and me going at it, Garrett. I'm feeling extremely Alpha all of a sudden, and being patient has never been part of that instinct, at least not for me. So tell me how long you'll be." Another growl came from Josh's core right then, deeper and more possessive than ever, one that lit Hayden up like a fireworks display. His whole body reacted, tensed as he caught a fresh waft of Josh's marking scent.

"Stop that," he warned in a thick voice, fumbling with his bootlaces. "Or I'll never make it home."

In a very firm voice, Josh issued one very powerful word—the most powerful word any Alpha could issue to another wolf. "Stay."

Hayden's blood ran even hotter at his lover's commanding tone. Planting his right palm on the mattress, Hayden leaned low and nuzzled Josh with a sweet, gentle kiss. Josh's tongue teased against his lips, his arms encircling Hayden's shoulders to bring him much closer. Then, with a soft rumble, Josh lapped at Hayden's cheek, nuzzling him back. Alpha to Alpha, they pressed their faces together, panting quickly.

Later, once they'd regained enough strength, they'd transform into their werewolf bodies and run together through the woods. Hayden's heart hammered at the thought, and he only wished he possessed enough strength to call forth his wolf form right now. There'd be no going home if he could, though, so perhaps it was for the best that he was forced to remain human for now.

Still, when they were strong enough to transform, they'd roam the valley, the streams, the mountains together, all the while feeling the heat of the moon's rays beating upon their sleek bodies. Hayden could barely wait to run wild with his mate.

Josh licked his throat with the tip of his tongue, making playful growling noises. "Stay," he repeated, tugging on Hayden's shoulders.

Hayden shook his head. "Can't, baby. But you tell me when you want me back here," Hayden groaned, "and this wolf will heel and comply."

"Now." Josh's reply was a throaty rumble. "I want you now, Alpha. But you head back to your parents' house 'cause you have to. Do your thing, then come right back home to me."

Hayden cuffed the back of Josh's nape with playful roughness. "An hour. Back in an hour."

Josh nuzzled him again, running both hands through Hayden's hair in a gesture of deep possession. "Too long. Faster."

"The only timetable I'm on is yours, baby, so I'll be quick." Hayden laughed, knowing he would have to be the disciplined and focused one. He rattled off his duty list with quick efficiency. "Jump in the shower, grab clothes, deal with folks, back in an hour...or less."

"Perfect timetable." Joshua collapsed onto his back with a frustrated groan of desire. Then he propped his head on one elbow, giving Hayden an aroused, sensual grin. "Just know that this bad wolf will be waiting for you, feeling very hungry indeed." He patted the empty place beside him on the bed. "And keeping the sheets warm."

Hayden remembered staring at him for one long, last moment, then hurrying out the door. The world had seemed more open, more rich than hours before. He'd left

Joshua's small, warm house whistling contentedly. He could remember tossing his car keys into the air, feeling the deepest, truest completion he'd ever known in his life. Feeling beautiful and sexy and loved.

He belonged to Josh, he'd thought, his entire body humming with the spiritual and physical connection that occurred when two wolves mated for life. I'm his—and he is mine, he'd marveled, heading out to his SUV. After that, everything in Hayden's mind turned as blank as a whiteout blizzard.

Timetable. The word clicked around in his head, familiar. Haunting. Timetable... The only timetable...

All at once, Hayden recalled Josh's words to him the other day. When he'd shown up the day after their meeting in the bar. Josh had held him from behind, promising to woo him, swearing that he'd make Hayden understand just how much Josh loved him. He'd whispered the words in Hayden's ear, brushing up against his nape like liquid heat.

The only timetable I'm on is yours. Timetable. The word echoed in his mind, haunting him, gaining painful new context. Joshua had repeated Hayden's very own words from all those years ago, obviously trying to jog some forgotten memory from Hayden's own mind.

Oh, God. Joshua had been referring to the night of their mating, a night Hayden had never remembered until now. What had Josh lived with, all these years, the memories alive and real to him? Knowing that those same experiences were all but dead to his mate?

It's okay, baby. I remember now, Hayden pledged his lover. I will remember all of it, I promise. And then I will come hunting and prowling...for you, my mate. Only for you.

Chapter Ten

Five years earlier, December 30th, shortly after six a.m.

The headlights of Hayden's SUV fanned across the remote two-lane, illuminating freshly fallen snow marked by a single set of tire tracks. The road was a remote one, a shortcut between the rural area where Josh lived and the more populated main highway to Jackson. Absently he wondered who else had traveled the same path at such an early hour on Sunday morning.

Lifting his coat sleeve to his nostrils, Hayden drank in Josh's scent, not surprised to discover that he was absolutely drenched in it—his mate had marked him from the crown of his head all the way to his toes. Smelling this strongly of another wolf, Hayden would be damned lucky if his dad didn't attack him from blind instinct before he'd even crossed the threshold to their home. It was in the nature of any male wolf to guard his den against predators, and with Hayden reeking of a rival clan's scent, his father might misinterpret that initially, so he needed a good strategy.

Damn, why hadn't he taken just a few minutes to shower? He'd been too hurried, too concerned about getting home before his parents woke, but now he couldn't help cursing his lack of planning. Hayden could only hope that his father slept through his own arrival, including the mating scents that were all over his body and clothes.

He was mentally rehearsing what he'd tell his dad when his thoughts were interrupted by unexpected movement about twenty yards ahead. Hayden squinted, making out the dark forms of what appeared to be two men standing on the roadside beside a rusty old clunker. Looked like an El Camino, with its squat size and long open bed. Maybe they'd broken down, he thought, slowing as he approached. He wondered if he would recognize them from around town, but couldn't make out any details of their features in the whitewash of headlights and stark snow.

Pulling closer, he began rolling down his passenger side window, but then experienced a dark kick of adrenaline. The two men moved forward and huddled their bodies together like a barrier, clearly hoping to conceal something. Only theirs was a feeble effort— Hayden instantly spotted a human body lying lifelessly on the snow beside their vehicle.

The rest happened in what felt like slow motion, an off-kilter, sinister kaleidoscope of imagery. His window on automatic, still sliding down; his foot hovering against the accelerator; the men glaring at him, eyes glowing in the headlights; the crumpled male form by their back tires; dark crimson splotches seeping into the snow.

From the corner of his eye, he saw the bigger of the

two men—a stringy-haired, bearded figure—move toward the passenger door of the vehicle. The other turned back toward the body as if he intended to move it.

Hayden gunned his SUV, heading toward a turn-around that he knew was only a few more yards ahead. He'd get to it, pull through, and drive back to the main highway as fast as possible given the road conditions. He focused on the road ahead, but then suddenly a pair of headlights popped to life in his rearview—the men were following him. His mind flashed on the image of the blood-soaked snow and dead body again—he had to get off this remote switchback road and fast. On instinct, he patted his jacket pocket, reaching for his cell phone, only to recall that he'd left it at home.

But then he thought of Josh waiting for him back in bed, sleeping beneath sheets that were strewn and rumpled from their lovemaking. Josh became Hayden's one beacon in the terrifying moment's reality, and although he knew the men were dangerous, he also knew that if he could just get back to Josh's house, they'd be able to call the cops. It was much farther to his parents' place, or even to any gas station. On this remote strip of road, his best hope was of returning to Josh. He pressed the pedal down with even more force, ignoring the way his rear tires chewed at the snow.

He hit the wheel on a hard right, his back tires fishtailing so badly that he nearly lost control of the SUV. Thankfully, he managed to make the turn without spinning out and then accelerated back toward the site. He swallowed hard as he prepared to pass the crime

scene a second time. There was no other way to safety—
not if he didn't want to lead the two thugs right to his own
parents—than driving past them a second time.

Up ahead, their own headlights grew larger, a blinding
swathe in the darkness. Hayden drove faster, praying the
men didn't have a gun they were aiming at him. A few
more seconds and their two vehicles would be passing
each other as they approached him at a thunderously fast
pace all their own.

He had to get back to Joshua, and fast. Suddenly the
five-minute drive to his mate seemed the longest of his
entire life. And he'd never yearned for Joshua Peterson
more than he did in that single heartbeat of a moment.

I should stop the car and transform. Go wolf and fight
these men, here and now.

For a moment, he took his foot off the pedal, reaching
for the hem of his sweatshirt. But then, with sickening
dread, he remembered that his wolf's defenses would be
useless to him. Now that the mating process had begun,
he'd be utterly unable to transform to wolf form for weeks.
Possibly until the next full moon. All his wolf's instincts
and nature were engaged in securing the bond with Josh.

Flexing his hands, wishing they were paws, Hayden
yearned for his werewolf nature more than he ever had
before. But it was lost to him right now. There was only
one choice, and although it was dangerous, he had to
take it.

Hayden sped down the long drive to Josh's house,
eyes locked on his rearview the entire time. By his

calculations, he only had a few seconds lead on the men who had followed him the entire returning distance. Slamming his SUV into park, he leapt out of the vehicle and scrambled up the back steps that led to Josh's kitchen back door.

"Josh!" he shouted as he tried the knob, praying that his mate hadn't locked the door behind him. Hayden hit full scale panic when the handle didn't budge and began pounding on the door with his fist, screaming for Josh to open up. All the while he kept his gaze turned sideways, watching for his pursuer's headlights.

And then he saw them, their icy silver illumination thrown up against the tall aspens that ran the back length of Josh's property. "Joshua," he screamed shrilly. "Open the fuck up! Josh!"

He heard stirring on the other side of the door, saw the spit of snow and dark tires round the corner of the house—only ten feet or so from where he stood. The door jerked open and he practically fell inside, atop Josh.

"What's going on? What's wrong?" Josh stared past Hayden, wide-eyed and confused. And totally naked, just like Hayden had left him.

"Lock it," he said breathlessly, slamming it himself. "No, go get something to barricade it. Get a phone. Do you have a gun?" He blurted more directions, hardly able to breathe, barely managing to explain what he'd come upon in his truck.

Josh was instantly on the other side of the kitchen, yanking open drawers and sending utensils flying. A thunderous pounding began on the other side of the door. Josh froze, long steak knife in his grasp, and Hayden paused right in front of the door. He hadn't even been given enough seconds to form an additional barricade. It wasn't exactly Fort Knox, either, and those violent men would easily be able to break down the door. Their only hope was if they could call the police and now.

Hayden's gaze locked like a laser on Josh, who stood silent and still on the other side of the room. Joshua's nakedness, so beautiful and arousing earlier, now made him seem brutally vulnerable, as if nothing would separate him from the murderers on the other side of the door. His mate was without even the most basic protection of clothing.

The door began to rock beneath physical blows from the outside, its thin wood bowing in the center. Hayden's eyes watered and his throat went dry. Never taking his gaze off of Josh, he asked in a still whisper. "Where's the phone? We've got to call the cops."

Josh pointed down the hallway and toward his bedroom. "Only have my cell," he whispered, his own eyes wide and bright. "It's in the bedroom."

"Go." Hayden gestured with his head, pushing both palms against the door—as if he could keep the men out as a mere human.

If only he had enough strength to turn wolf, but he didn't. His internal energy was too spent; no way did he have the kind of primal power to transform, not after such intense mating.

"Hayden, I can't leave you here," Josh told him, his tone raw and protective. His mate took several steps toward the door, but all Hayden could focus on was how naked and vulnerable he looked.

"Get the fuck back to your room, Josh! Now! Call the cops. I'll keep them at bay long as I can."

Josh sprang toward him, pressing the kitchen knife into Hayden's hand. "This is all I've got. No guns. I don't have the strength the transform..."

"Neither of us do, not right now." Hayden pulled Josh close, needing to hold his mate, if only for a moment. "I'm going to protect you, baby."

"We fight together," Josh insisted, stepping out of Hayden's brief embrace.

Hayden thought of the dead body he'd seen in the snow, the pool of red blood beneath it; then he pictured the two men on the other side of the door. He braced both forearms against the wooden frame, ready to fight, even if only with his human strength.

"Call the police, Joshua," he instructed as calmly as possible. "Then lock yourself in your bedroom. And don't come out, no matter what happens or what you hear. Stay in there, okay?"

"No fucking way!" Josh sprinted down the hall, calling over his shoulder. "I'm not locking you out, Hayden. I'm coming right back."

The door splintered into pieces at that precise moment, a meaty fist reaching through and grabbing Hayden's throat before he could recoil from where he stood.

"Open the goddamned door," the attacker who held him spat, slamming Hayden's forehead against the solid part of the wood as he spoke. Immediately Hayden's vision swam, making it impossible to get a good look at the man who held him. But he could smell the rancid breath and stale cigarette smoke that went with the voice. Hayden tried to jab his knife at the man, but the weapon was wrestled from his grasp.

"I'm...not making this easy for you," Hayden spat back and was immediately punished with another slamming blow of his head against the frame, as well as a tightening grip around his throat. He pictured Josh, how naked and exposed he'd been.

Get dressed, Josh, he thought. Put clothes on for this fight.

He wasn't sure why, but instinct told him it was very important that Josh not be naked when these men got to him. Another hand came through the gap, reaching through and unlocking the door and Hayden was sent sprawling backward. He landed on the floor beside the hallway right as the men burst inside practically atop him. In that chilling moment of violence, the thing he noticed most of all was the frigid air from outside, hitting him like a solid wall...and that one man was already moving into the hallway, closer toward Joshua. Driven by a mate's instincts, he leaped to his feet and barreled into that man, body slamming him against the wall. There was a moment, a slow-motion, surreal one, where that assailant gaped back at Hayden, too stunned to move.

And Hayden seized that split-second window of time to make his move.

He sprinted down the hall, intent on protecting Josh and making sure that he could complete the call to the police. But the minute he entered the bedroom, he realized the authorities weren't coming. It was too late for help. The cell phone lay in shards against the wall, where presumably it had been flung by the thug who now pinned Josh against that same wall.

"Let him go," Hayden said in a voice of forced calm. "He's not part of this. He didn't see what I did. Leave him be."

The man turned chilling, lifeless eyes on Hayden right then. They reminded him of a coyote's yellow, ancient gaze, boring into Hayden with pure evil intent. "Well, well, well," the man said, his long, stringy hair falling across those eyes. "Look what we got here. A pair of queers, huh? That why you were on that road at this time of morning...that why this one here's naked and shivering? 'Cause you're his lover?" He spat that last word at Hayden, still staring, and then slowly turned his attention back to Josh. The man kept Josh pinned by the throat, the Alpha's back pressed against the wall. Josh never so much as flinched despite his captor's tight grip around his throat.

The man leered at Josh. "You queers make me wanna be sick. Here I was worried about what your boyfriend over there saw, and I get the chance to do a little housecleaning for the state of Wyoming. My lucky day, isn't it?"

The assailant's companion appeared in the doorway. "They're the only ones here. Nobody else."

"Two pretty boys shacking up together, out here in God's country. Can you believe it?" The man snarled. "We got us a pair of faggots."

"No, we are not," Josh said coolly, eyes locked right on the face of the man who held him.

"I can smell his sex all over you, boy." The stringy-haired man sniffed Josh's face and Hayden wanted to growl and leap, needed to bare teeth at the man who threatened his mate. Flexing both hands, he sought to summon his wolf's form, but it remained dormant because he was still too weak to make the change.

"Don't you touch him," Hayden seethed, yearning to feel the prickling of fur along his chest.

In answer, the fat man jammed a gun up beneath Josh's chin. "Like this?" He laughed. "You mean, I shouldn't get my pistol ready?"

Behind him, Hayden heard the other man—the one who was tall and skinny—chuckle low in his throat. "Yeah," the skinny man drawled, "something tells me you'd like to use your gun on that fellow, Rawlings."

Rawlings. A name. Only, having it didn't give Hayden hope at all, didn't offer the promise of turning these men into the cops once they'd had their fun. It told him they didn't plan to let either of them walk away this night.

Hayden dropped his head low and began growling like any wolf would if his mate were threatened. The man with the stringy hair laughed again, the dirty sound he emitted more a drunken gurgle than a mirthful one. "Getting all proprietary, huh?" He taunted as Hayden's growl grew louder. "You think this boy's all yours? You think I can't fuck him, too?"

When Hayden didn't answer, he received a punishing roundhouse to the right jaw. His eyeglasses went flying against the bookshelf, and fell to the floor with a clatter. The big man stepped on them, grinding them beneath his boot. He stepped closer to Hayden, but kept his gun trained on Joshua. "You think I can't do whatever the fuck I want with your boy now, you pansy?" The man chuckled, the rolling sound as wet and humorless as before. He gave his pal a disgusted glance, nodding with a sneer. "Yep, faggots for sure."

Then their captor spat in Josh's direction, missing his target, yet explaining his intention nonetheless. Josh never so much as flinched, standing naked at gunpoint. "Tie him up good, right on the bed. Use the four posters," he barked, eyes ratcheted on Josh. "I'll show 'em what we think of faggots, all right. What we do when they get out of line. By the time I'm done, these boys won't squeal a word. Not to the police, not to nobody."

"And you?" The bastard taunted Hayden, his choking grip growing even tighter about Hayden's throat. "You're gonna watch the whole goddamned show."

He nodded toward Josh again, and with his right hand, the assailant began unfastening his own belt. The movement caused Hayden's own head to bob against his will. With a scowl, as if he disapproved of Hayden's subtle movement, the assailant grabbed a chunk of Hayden's

154

hair, yanking his head back with such force, it slammed against the wall. Hayden heard the cracking thud as if it were on delay, a half-second out of sync with the action itself. His eyes filled with bright, descending lights and he felt his body pull downward, too.

No, he told himself. Joshua's life depends on me. I must protect my mate. Even if I die in the process, I must save him!

Hayden lunged, his wolf's power surging forth from deep inside—every primal instinct awakened, giving him the supernatural strength required to save his mate. Only...he still couldn't transform. The power just wasn't there as he reached for it, but he'd be damned if they'd touch Joshua for another moment. If he'd let them do what they'd threatened to do to his mate. Whatever it took, however possible—if he had to die in the process— he would overpower these men before they harmed Josh.

Hayden spun, kneeing his captor in the groin, then with a twisting maneuver, sprang free, slamming his other attacker against the bedroom wall. The creep grunted, stunned for a moment, his soot-gray eyes widening in surprise. And then he grinned, revealing yellow, gapped teeth; Hayden got a sick feeling as he turned to follow the man's gaze, realizing he'd had something concealed behind his back.

That something was a thick lead pipe swinging toward Hayden's head. The club-like weapon cut through the air. Forceful. Erratic. As surgical as a baseball bat about to connect with a fastball.

Hayden's world went black a millisecond later.

"Fucking faggots. Always causing trouble." The words were grunted against Josh's nape, mixed with the scent of beer and stale cigarettes and old sweat. Josh tried turning his head to bite or spit at his assailant, but his face was pressed into the mattress too forcefully.

Hayden. He had to know if Hayden was still alive.

He ignored the ripping pain, the invasion, the filthy feeling of what was being done to him—the shame of those groping, rough hands. He was numb, on another plane, drifting. The only image or physical sensation he allowed to penetrate him belonged to Hayden.

Hayden holding him earlier. Hayden sliding between his legs, so gentle. The long strokes of those graceful, large hands.

The feel of Hayden's full, sweet mouth against his own.

Darker thoughts swam over those, drowning them. Hayden being bludgeoned...over and over. Hayden crumpling against the bookshelves, lovely blue eyes rolling back in his head, then closing. The heavy pipe cracking into his skull, blood all over the handsome face that Josh now dearly loved.

And then, finally, the pistol—the black-bellied weapon cocked against his mate's temple. The threats that if Josh fought at all, then the trigger would be pulled. Hayden would die for sure then...if he wasn't gone already.

"Facedown," he'd been told. "You do as I say and he won't die." Then gritty rude laughter. "You won't ever say shit, neither, once we're done. You'll know what I'm capable of and you'll keep our secrets. I'm gonna make sure of that, pretty boy."

His wolf's nature howled silently, screaming for revenge, yet he remained unable to transform. At least for now...

They can touch me, but they'll never have me, he told himself, hips slamming into the mattress once again. I am Hayden Garrett's. They can't touch me, not really. He kept the mantra going, transporting his thoughts and body to another realm. Leaving the brutal moment's reality, he tried to remember the sweet taste of whiskey and Hayden's mouth. He tried to detect his mate's marking scent in the garish swill of stale cigarettes and sweat.

He tried to believe that Hayden's heart still beat, that his body and soul still lived.

They forced him to dress afterward, shoving him toward the back steps while hauling Hayden's unconscious form along with them. Dimly he thought they'd be dumped in the woods somewhere, their pitiful bodies left to freeze. No one would find them until spring thawed the ground to a sodden, dark pulp. Josh was startled when the ringleader shoved something at him. It took a moment for him to realize it was his own set of keys. "Here," the man ordered, pushing him toward the driver's side of the truck. "Get in."

Josh blinked, weaving on his feet unsteadily. His whole body burned and ached. "What...for?" he asked numbly.

"Get the fuck in, that's what. You do as you're told," the man barked with a lascivious grin. "Or hadn't you figured that part out yet?"

With a stumbling gait, Josh managed to reach his truck and after a couple of tries got the door to the cab open. For a long moment, he braced both palms against the driver's seat, trying to gather enough strength to climb up into the thing. Finally he managed to crawl inside, even as weak as he was and with as much pain as he currently felt. His stomach roiled and he thought he might retch up the whiskey from earlier, but he willed the sensation away, turning the key in the ignition.

The passenger door opened, and he was shocked when one of the men—he couldn't see which—deposited Hayden in the seat and slammed the door. Hayden crumpled sideways, slumping lifelessly in Josh's direction. Josh began reaching for his lover, desperate to know if he was alive, but a beefy hand seized his nape.

"No, shithead, you drive. Leave him be." It was the stringy-haired man who'd raped him, and feeling those hands on him again almost made Josh retch. The man leered at him and continued, "You gonna follow me. Do as I say. One wrong turn, and we're hunting your ass down. First thing we'll do, too, is finish off your lover boy. Understand?"

With a barking order, the skinny man searched the glove compartment and the truck's interior for any cell phone or communication devices. Satisfied that Josh was, in fact, marooned within his own pickup, they locked him inside with one last warning that he do as instructed, and then slammed the door. But not before the stringy-haired one cocked a gun, aiming it at Josh's mate, just to make his threatening point even more clear.

It wasn't exactly as if Josh could've evaded them or arrived at a brilliant escape strategy, even if he'd tried to. It took all his remaining strength just to keep from passing out cold behind the wheel. He moved the truck into gear and leaned forward in an effort to stay alert, and with his one free hand began feeling for Hayden. He made physical contact and with a frantic patting of his right hand, felt for Hayden's wrist, still just struggling to stay conscious. At last he had hold of that tender place where his mate's pulse either would—or wouldn't—be beating. Pressing it between his thumb and forefinger, Josh held his breath...and began weeping uncontrollably as he felt a weak, faint flutter between his fingertips.

Hayden was alive. Just barely, it seemed, but he was still alive.

They'd pulled to a stop on a remote switchback road, a curving bit of snow-dense highway. The lonely stretch would be treacherous even under much better conditions. It was still dark, although any minute and light would begin to touch the sky beyond the mountains. Their plan, they'd explained to Josh in cold, even tones, was for him to have an "accident" on the road, one that would involve running over the man they'd apparently murdered.

"Your buddy made the mistake of coming upon our clean-up job earlier. That's why he raced back to you."

Hayden had shouted something about the men being killers, and now Josh understood as he saw them spread a man's lifeless form in the middle of the road. They intended to make it look as if Josh had run him over, here on the dark, snowy road. The side door was yanked open by the man who'd raped him, those harsh eyes filled with what looked like amusement as he glanced down at Hayden's slumped form. "Yeah, he's almost dead anyway. This little car trip won't be any big thing, not now."

The man tossed the bottle of whiskey into the truck, top off, and it splashed across Hayden's pants and the floorboard. "Like the commercials say, drinking and driving is always a bad thing," he said with a sneer. "Now drive. Get this done right the first time, and you won't see me again."

With that, he slammed the door and then stood to the side, arms folded. Waiting.

Josh blinked, a sticky, thick substance preventing him from opening his eyes. His head felt as if someone had ripped it in half and he couldn't remember where he was or why his entire body ached. Something warm and soft was tangled up against him, and his feet seemed to be up over his head.

The smell of gasoline filled his nostrils, acrid and threatening. All at once, he jolted to alertness, remembering what had happened. They'd gone over the side of the mountain—he had lost control of the truck after carrying out his attackers' "orders".

"Hayden! Oh, God, baby." He tried to sit up, but the truck had flipped and they were upside down. He reached for Hayden, who was unconscious just as he had been before. Surely he was alive. Surely he was still breathing. With desperate, shaking hands, Josh felt for his lover's wrist once again, knowing that if he didn't find a pulse, he would die, too. In his soul.

Hayden's hand was covered in blood. Where was Hayden bleeding? Josh wondered in a panic, only to realize the blood had come from his own sticky hand. His own injuries were irrelevant, though, because the only thing that mattered was the reedy, thin pulse he felt beneath his fingertips.

"Hayden," he murmured, beginning to sob. "I'm going to get you out of this. I'm going to save you and protect you. I promise you, baby." He pressed a kiss to Hayden's battered temple and murmured the words as a heartfelt pledge. Somehow, despite their remote location—despite all that had been done to them—he would make sure his mate was safe. Not just from the night's violence, but for all time.

Chapter Eleven

Present day

Hayden approached the small house that Kira shared with her brother. Even though he'd never been back to the place since that fated night five years earlier, he was well aware that she'd moved in with Josh shortly after all the shit came down. And had never moved out. Staying on, he guessed, to make sure Josh ate decent meals between shifts. Thank God he'd had her, Hayden thought, his chest tightening at the thought of how much his mate had suffered in the past five years.

He pulled down the wooded drive that wound to the back of the house, and released a sigh of relief when he spotted Kira's pickup truck. Inspecting himself in the rearview mirror, he hated how haggard he looked, too thin after the weeks spent in wolf form. Running quick hands over his hair, he smoothed it one more time and, heart jackhammering, stepped out of the SUV.

Slowly he approached the back steps to the house, memories flashing through his mind like strobe lights. A blinding headache began pounding behind his eyes as he saw himself racing up these same steps, remembered the crippling fear he'd experienced as the men had followed him into the driveway. He stopped, unable to walk forward for a moment as he felt their rough hands on him...and saw those same rough hands manhandling Josh.

He pressed a hand to his eyes, moaning low in his throat—then growling as he kept seeing the violent bastards, kept remembering how they'd harmed his mate. "No," he swore in a guttural tone, burying his face in both hands. "It's all in the past."

"But Joshua needs you now."

Kira's unexpected words jolted him, making him yelp slightly in surprise. Dropping his hands away from his face, he found her standing inside the door, holding it open for him. Bright, cheery light spilled out from the kitchen behind her, making it hard to read her features, but he'd have sworn she wore a shocked expression.

"How could you stay away like this? For so long?" Kira demanded quietly, still standing in the open kitchen door. "Don't you know how it's been killing him?"

Her words were a quiet accusation, and Hayden hung his head. Yes, he was well aware that the past few weeks must have taken a harsh toll on Josh, but they'd been necessary.

She stared down at him. "He's convinced you're dead, Hayden. That's how bad the situation is. How bad of a shape he's gotten himself into."

"It killed me, too. Keeping away from him, but I had to reclaim my memories. It was the only way we could have a future together." Hayden stared past her, into the house's warm interior. He kept looking up at those welcoming kitchen lights, hating that a simple house could fill him with so much terror and dread—even as it reawakened memories of his mating night, of falling deeply in love.

Kira planted hands on her hips, clearly prepared to confront him. "Are you back for good now, Hayden? Because if you're not ready to be with Josh—really be with him—then you better stay away," she persisted. "I don't think he could handle you showing up and taking off again. I really don't."

He swallowed, feeling his eyes burn. "I...I haven't gone to him yet."

"He won't be home for another three hours. He's still at the station."

"I know. I drove by there like...damn, at least ten times trying to get up the nerve to go inside, and that's when I realized I had to come here."

"You're going to wait for him to get back? Because I can call him, and he'd be out of there in a heartbeat."

"I came to talk to you."

Kira blinked at him and gave a slow nod. "You have questions."

"I have to know if what I remember...if it's..."

"Hayden, it's all true. It all happened." She stared at him for a significant, penetrating moment, making it very clear that her brother had confided everything about that night. "I'm sorry," she said softly, "but the past you shared with my brother...the things that happened, they're harsh. And they're real. Very real."

He swallowed hard, staring at the ground. He had to confirm everything, all the terrible memories he'd reclaimed. Clearing his throat, he pressed, "But Josh, did they..." Oh, God, he couldn't bring himself to say it aloud, but Kira was just staring, waiting, almost as if she wanted to force the words out of him. Perhaps she did.

He dropped his voice to a whisper. "Did they harm him...sexually? Did they do that to my mate?"

Kira met his gaze boldly and said, "You tried to stop it, and they beat you with a lead pipe. Over and over again, while Josh was forced to watch. And when they thought you were dead—when Josh thought so, too—they turned their full attention to him."

Hayden began shaking, fists forming in rage. He felt fur prickle across his chest, and couldn't stop the threatening growls that rumbled forth from his center.

"Like I told you, Hayden," she said quietly. "All of it's true. Now go to him."

"Or wait here?" he asked.

"Just be with him. Herc, there, whatever," she said. "But don't make him wait any more."

Josh stared at the sheaf of paperwork on his desk, but didn't really see any of it. His mind was filled with other images, ones that plagued him nonstop, night and day, and pursued him with ravenous strength. Well, it was mostly one horrifying image: Hayden in wolf form, dead in the snow, frozen hard like the cold earth beneath him.

Yeah, Josh was losing it, for sure. He raked a hand over his tired, bleary eyes, and bent over his desk. Paperwork. He hoped the mundane task would help keep his fears from gnawing him alive. As he hunched forward, pen in hand, a massive shadow filled his open office door. He recognized the man without even looking up. Nobody around the station loomed nearly as large as Ben Orson did.

Nor did any of the others try to get in his business like Ben, either. For some reason the big grizzly of a man always came pawing around, even when all of Josh's other friends in the department knew to give him a wide berth like they did right now. He'd heard them muttering under their breath out at the coffee machine. "Peterson's in a shit mood. I'd steer clear."

"'Sup, Ben?" Josh kept his gaze fixed on the paperwork, throwing off a seriously uninviting vibe.

He heard slow, purposeful footsteps until Ben stood right in front of him, forcing Josh to look up at him. "What's up?" Josh repeated.

Ben cracked a lazy smile, folding massive forearms over his chest. "Just making sure you're still alive in here, that's all, Sarge."

"Working," Josh barked, bending back over the desk dismissively. "Just working. Which might be a good thing for you to go do, right, Orson?"

But Ben didn't move. Instead, he bent down, planted massive, paw-like hands on the edge of the desk, and in a barely audible voice announced, "He's still alive."

Josh jerked back in his chair, eyes going wide and heart pounding. "Wh-what did you just say?"

Ben kept his posture low, dark eyes locking with Josh's intently, and said nothing until very slowly he smiled. And then he stood upright again, turned and lumbered out of the office without another word.

He's still alive. Still. Alive.

How did Ben know about Hayden? The cop wasn't a werewolf. He was only human—and it wasn't common knowledge anywhere around town that Josh was gay or had a lover, much less one who'd been missing for almost seven weeks.

What exactly was Ben Orson? More importantly, were the man's words correct?

For the first time in weeks, Josh's heart surged and pumped with hope that his mate might still find his way home.

Josh pulled up his cruiser in front of Hayden's dark house, parking on the snow-covered drive. This was his nightly drill, to swing by and check on the place. To make sure his mate's home remained secure, even as he desperately prayed that this time when he approached he would finally see lights on inside.

However, as always since Hayden had split, no dice. Josh's hope sank heavily, like a stone in the river that ran behind the little fishing cottage. For a long moment, he remained inside the vehicle, replaying Ben Orson's words from earlier in the evening.

He's still alive.

The sentence bounced around in his mind causing a dim flare of optimism—one that Josh wanted to outright curse himself for entertaining. For all he knew, Ben had just been talking shit or trying to get a rise out of him. Still, why would he have chosen those particular words? And why would Ben, one of the quietest, steadiest men he knew, ever play with Josh's head?

None of the gang at the station knew about Hayden, anyway. Well, no one other than the chief himself, and he was a sealed vault when it came to secrets or confessions, especially of the damningly personal kind. The man had never revealed the truth about what went down on that December night five years ago, or about Josh being gay. Not any of it, and there was no reason to think he'd start now.

Josh blew out a bone-weary sigh and slowly reached to open the cruiser's door. Easing his boots out into the snow-covered drive, his wolf instincts fired up immediately, almost at the same time as his cop ones did. There were fresh prints in the snow, and the very strong scent of a fellow wolf permeated the air.

He froze, the swell of hope and longing that filled him now so strong that it nearly paralyzed him. Oh, by God, he recognized the scent, so familiar and gorgeous. So vivid and vital. Hayden was alive and nearby, so close Josh might actually find him.

Instantly Josh went rock hard inside his uniform pants, his body reacting on every level. He caught his own mating scent as it wafted off his skin, felt his erection grow thick and tight and hot as it pressed against his fly. His eyes narrowed, his pulse went electric.

But more than any of his instinctive reactions to having caught his mate's scent trail, it was the way his chest grew tight as a drum that most affected him, the yearning nearly dropping him to his knees. Oh, God, how he'd missed his lover, how he'd longed to—just once more in his life—smell the heady, powerful scent of the Alpha who was somewhere nearby and meant everything to him.

His whole body shaking, Josh stepped fully out of the vehicle, scanning the dark perimeter with his heightened wolf's vision and sniffing at the air. He walked as if on autopilot, clenching and unclenching his fists against his upper thighs, hardly daring to hope despite his body's primal reaction. One foot after the other he moved, following the trail that grew more overpowering as he rounded the left side of the fishing shack.

All at once, he heard a low, guttural growl. The hair on his nape bristled and he whipped his head in the direction of the sound. There on the small deck that ran along the back of Hayden's home, lined in silver moonlight, was the only wolf he'd ever wanted. The one he'd dreamed and prayed to find again. Hayden stood on the railing, his wolf's chest thrust outward, his blue eyes ferociously narrow, his silver coat gleaming.

Oh, God, he's feral. He's alive, but he's fully wolf, lost to me, Josh thought, feeling tears sting his eyes. *It's too*

169

late now.

Josh could barely breathe at all, transfixed by the low growling noise the other Alpha emitted. Not wanting to send him running into the woods all over again.

"Hayden," he murmured softly, touching his own chest. "It's me. It's Joshua. You're safe with me."

I have to change, Josh decided in a panic, I have to become wolf myself so he won't bolt.

But before Josh had time to move a muscle toward transformation, Hayden leaped off that railing, bounding across the snow toward him at a lightning-fast run. Josh braced, preparing for the attack, ripping at his uniform so he could transition—and was knocked flat on his back when Hayden pounced at him with the force of a hurricane.

Josh thrust a protective arm upward, wrestling with the other wolf, ready to fling him off...but was stunned when a rough, lapping tongue began licking at his cheeks, working at the tears he hadn't realized were streaming down his face. He slid his fingers through the soft, warm fur that covered him from face to hips, rubbing, feeling. The wolf atop him whined lightly, snuffling his nose against the column of Josh's throat.

Then another shocking change—and it was Hayden in human form, spread atop him, naked. It was Hayden kissing Josh's face, licking away the tears that simply wouldn't be stopped.

"I'm here, baby," his lover murmured, finding Josh's mouth with his own. "It's okay. I'm here, and I'm not going anywhere...not ever again."

Josh's tears turned to sobs, and he wrapped both arms about Hayden's bare body.

Hayden led the way inside his house, Josh on his heels. He closed the door and locked it, neither of them uttering a word. In fact, Josh hadn't spoken at all since Hayden had jumped him out in the snow. The only sounds he'd made had been wrenching sobs as Hayden had licked and kissed away every tear, murmuring promises over and over. That he would never leave Joshua again, and that he'd spend the rest of their lives doing his level best to heal his mate's broken heart.

Reaching to flip on the hallway light, Hayden suddenly felt Josh grabbing him from behind. Those strong hands weren't gentle as they seized hold of Hayden's forearms, flipping him face-forward. And Josh was just all on him, pushing him hard with his own body, backing Hayden up against the wall until his bare back met the rough wooden texture with a forceful shove.

Josh said nothing, his only sound a low, angry growl as he flattened Hayden against the log beams, framing him between forearms that he braced on both sides of Josh's face. Josh lowered his head, still growling as he sniffed Hayden's naked body, inspecting Hayden like a potential predator—as if it were the only way to be sure Hayden was truly himself.

Hayden kept still, silent, even when Josh thrust his hips up close, aggressively pinning Hayden against the wall with his groin. With an erection so hard and thick, Hayden began shaking from unspent hunger for the man who held him captive. Five years had been far, far too long, and now? Standing naked and feeling his mate's pulsing cock shoved against his own groin? He thickened, an instant, unstoppable reaction to such intimate, physical contact. The warm skin of his exposed cock scraped against the fabric of Josh's uniform pants, and as he lengthened, Hayden attempted to shift his hips to accommodate the change—but Josh wouldn't budge, keeping him pinioned with his own hips so that Hayden's hard-on pushed against his mate's own rigid erection. Hayden nearly came as their groins pushed and bulged together so harshly, skin against fabric, heat against heat.

"Joshua," he moaned with a ragged, desperate plea. "Touch me. Let me hold you."

Hayden lifted both hands, about to cup Josh's face in his hands, but his mate ducked his head away, and Hayden let his hands fall back to his sides. Whatever Josh was doing right now, it was somehow critical to healing their ruptured mating bond—to drawing them back together.

Josh stopped growling. He pressed his nose against Hayden's neck, sniffing, then moved all along Hayden's face and bare shoulders—and back behind his ear. Josh kept inhaling Hayden's scent the entire time, inspecting, obviously needing to make sure that Hayden wasn't some figment of the other Alpha's imagination. Wanting to confirm that Hayden truly had returned from the wild.

"It's really me, baby," Hayden finally whispered,

daring to lift his hand again and touch Josh's cheek. His mate flinched, jerking back, but kept both forearms in locked position around Hayden's own face. Hayden felt the rough fabric of Josh's police uniform, the starched sleeves brushing his unshaven cheeks.

"Joshua, it's okay," he tried quietly. "I'm back. It's me. You can see that it's me."

"I can smell that it's you, too," Josh agreed hoarsely. "But I don't understand."

"Don't understand what?" Hayden stared at his mate, but Josh avoided his gaze, keeping his eyes fixed on the wall beyond Hayden's right shoulder.

When Josh remained silent, Hayden tried again. "Baby, tell me what you don't understand," he urged.

Finally, after a long, silent moment, Josh blew out a sigh and leveled Hayden with a firm, hard gaze. "My mate would never have left me for such a long time," Josh said in a voice like gravel. "My mate...knows I love him. My mate knows this in his heart, would always know this in his soul, even if he couldn't remember the truth. My mate," Josh said in a raw, broken tone, "would never have left me for weeks to wonder if he was alive or if I'd ever see him again at all. No, my mate wouldn't leave me alone and hurting...like you did."

Hayden's eyes slid shut and he felt the burn of tears. "I didn't remember. I had to know. Had to figure it out for myself. It was the only way we could have a future, for me to remember it all."

Josh reached a shaking hand toward Hayden's face,

capturing a long lock of Hayden's dark hair between his fingertips. Slowly Josh lifted it to his nose, testing even that scent. Then after a moment, Josh brought the lock to his lips, kissing it softly as he squeezed his eyes closed. "You are Hayden Garrett," he whispered as if satisfied by the inspection. "You are still my mate, even if my marking scent isn't on you after so many years."

"It is me, and I won't ever hurt you like again," Hayden promised fiercely, reaching to pull Josh into his arms, but the other wolf jerked away, stepping back by several paces until they were physically separated. The pain and anger in his magnetic eyes was visible even by the moonlight spilling through the room's windows.

"Everything I did," Josh said slowly, "every choice I made was always to protect you. Don't you love me at least a little bit in return?" Josh's voice was so broken, so destroyed—the words uttered from such clear, brutal pain—that Hayden literally wavered on his feet.

But only for a moment. Then he moved to Joshua and slowly knelt before his mate as if his very body were an offering. A pledge of love and fidelity, of worship. Taking both of Josh's rough hands in his own, he pressed them to his cheeks. "Joshua, you are the love of my life. You're all I ever wanted, all I ever will want. Don't you know that?"

He didn't dare look up, didn't even wait for a reply, just let the words come tumbling out of him in a torrent. "You are how I knew I was gay...why I knew I could never want any woman. Because of how badly I wanted you, all the way back in high school. I never got to tell you that, we were separated too soon..." Hayden kept his eyes shut tight, just letting the words spill out, vaguely aware that tears now streamed down his cheeks, dampening Josh's hands that he still held tight against his face. "I mean, you figured out that I wanted you, I could never hide that, obviously. But the way I wanted you, it was like a fever, even when I was just sixteen years old. While the other guys were all after some girl or another, it was you I thought about all the time. Damn, being on the football team with you, playing baseball together, and seeing you naked in the showers? Watching you change clothes in the locker room, and burning for you but not being able to do a damned thing about it? It was enough to make me crazy. That's why I picked Dartmouth—so far from our own land—because I thought maybe then I could find a way to forget you. Find a way to get past my fever." Hayden laughed softly. "God, I actually believed those thousands of miles between us would help. That they would succeed in driving you from my mind, my heart." Hayden shook his head slowly. "None of it ever did any good. You were inside me, down deep in my bones, living in my skin right along with me. You always have been...you still are. You'll always be inside of me, beating like my own heart, flowing like my own blood. That's what a mate does. It's who you are to me...the best of me."

Slowly he dared to tilt his head upward and look at Josh, praying that he would glimpse forgiveness, see that Josh believed in his love. As he did so, Josh dropped down to his own knees, pressing his forehead against Hayden's. For a moment, neither spoke, and then Josh moved his face slightly, until they were cheek to cheek, and he slid strong, muscular arms about Hayden.

"Did it ever occur to you," Josh whispered into his ear, "that if you'd stuck around Jackson, you might've made me fall in love with you sooner?" Josh kissed him slowly on the cheek, moving his mouth back to Hayden's ear as he added, "And if you'd just kissed me the first time we went on that run together after your freshman year, I'd have followed you all the way back to New Hampshire and nothing would've ever kept me away."

Hayden buried his face against Josh's shoulder, feeling the rough starch of his uniform. "I loved you...while I was in prison. I was just crazy in love with you, Joshua. Even after I got out, I still loved you, but I didn't understand why I'd fallen so much harder than before. Why my fever had grown when all I could remember was that kiss."

"You didn't know we'd mated, couldn't remember any of it."

Hayden closed his eyes, hating what he was about to ask, but he had to. "Why didn't you tell me the truth? Why didn't you come to me, soon as I was out of the coma, and make me remember everything?"

Josh tightened his arms around him, holding him even closer. Hayden could feel the rapid rhythm of his mate's heart, sensed its tempo increase as he answered, "Do you remember the men? Rawlings and Keener? Do you recall seeing them dump that body...any of it?"

Hayden sucked in a tight breath. "Josh, I remember it

all. I remember...everything."

Josh stiffened against him, a small shudder echoing through his body. And he hated the shame that he sensed in his mate. "It's okay," Hayden soothed softly. "It's all right, Joshua. I only regret that I couldn't protect you...that I didn't. A mate always protects his beloved."

Josh released him, leaning back on his heels with a long, penetrating gaze. "That is exactly why I didn't tell you the truth about us. That is why I let you go to prison. It was the only place where I could be sure they wouldn't try and harm you. If you were locked away, you were locked away from them, from their gang. Or at least that's what I hoped...even though I knew they might have people in there, too."

"We could have gone after them together, gotten our packs together."

Josh shook his head forcefully, but said nothing.

"Seriously, Josh, we could have taken them down...you didn't have to suffer so much by yourself. You bore all of it on your own shoulders—"

"Tate Rawlings came to me the first night you were in the hospital. He told me that if I ever told anything about that night—if I ever told you the truth when you woke up—that he'd kill you himself. That if I talked to the police, he would go up to the intensive care ward and make sure your life support was disconnected...that if you woke and left the hospital, he'd hunt you down. That he'd have someone else do the deed if I put him in prison by talking. He made one thing—one very definite point—

abundantly clear, and repeated it until I put him away...that he would see you dead if the truth ever came out." Josh raked a trembling hand over his brow. "That's why I said you were the one driving, even though you weren't.

"You see, Hayden, I didn't care about what he did to me. It was you. I didn't want him to touch you ever again, not like he'd touched me...not to end your life. Nothing. I would die myself to prevent it, and in a way, I did. Until I knew they were both behind bars and that I had a chance of winning you back, I was stone cold dead inside. Those five years, knowing what I'd done to your future, knowing that you believed I'd set you up...living without you...it was worse than I could have imagined. I felt, in a lot of ways, that I truly was dead."

Hayden reached forward, pulling Josh into his arms. "You're not alone anymore. You'll never be alone again. Whatever happens to us...it happens to both of us. Never alone again. You've got to promise me that. Whatever comes our way...good or bad, we face it together."

After a moment, Josh released a long, slow sigh. As if he'd unshouldered a great burden, as if a soothing sense of peace were settling over him. "I want you to know something," Josh said softly. "It's important that you know...I never slept with anyone else. I've been totally faithful to you."

Hayden suddenly remembered all those women from the bars, the ones he'd seen Josh kissing and cruising around with. Josh seemed to follow his thoughts because he said, "I had to keep some pretty rough company while doing undercover work. You saw that, I know...because I saw you watching sometimes."

"I was insanely jealous of those women," Hayden admitted, holding Josh even tighter. "I wanted to climb the fucking walls whenever I saw you with anyone."

"A mate's possessiveness," Josh agreed, nuzzling him.

"How'd you handle knowing I was supposedly single? That I thought I was?" Hayden asked, cringing as he thought of the fact that he had taken occasional lovers since their last time together. Nobody special; no one with forever stamped on their forehead, but he'd not gone five years without sex.

Josh growled and in a graceful movement had Hayden on his back, straddling him. "Don't ever mention that to me again," he said roughly. "I knew you'd have lovers, but I told myself that none of them would ever touch you like I had."

Hayden smiled slowly, sliding both hands to Josh's waist. "A cop on top. Now this is every gay man's fantasy—complete with uniform and weapons." He fingered Josh's badge, flicking it with his fingers. "Very hot, baby."

Josh didn't laugh or smile. His eyes narrowed as he stared down at Hayden, his chest heaving with quick pants. He was clearly upset by the mention of Hayden being with other men during the past five years, but Hayden wasn't going to let him focus on that fact. He slid a couple of fingers beneath the buttons of Josh's uniform shirt, and popped them loose.

Then stroking his hard, firm abdomen, Hayden moved to the next lower button. "Although I love the uniform, Joshua, I love the idea of stripping you out of it even more. But only if you're game...and I will be very gentle, I promise." Slowly he eased his hand lower, moving toward the decided ridge in the front of Josh's pants, but suddenly his lover flinched.

Hayden frowned as he recalled how Josh had been abused. That he'd never been touched out of love again in more than five years made his chest tighten and ache.

"Joshua, you know...actually, I think tonight we should just get reacquainted. Hold each other a while, maybe do a little kissing here and there, but nothing too overwhelming, not tonight," he said, cupping Josh's hips in both palms. "We're going to work our way up to making love again. It'll be like our very first time when it finally happens, but I'm going slow with you, Joshua. Slow and gentle and loving."

Josh's chest rose and fell even more quickly, and suddenly he leaned forward, splaying both palms on Hayden's chest. "Would you hold me? All night, until the sun rises, Hayden, please...just hold me."

"I'll hold you, Joshua, and watch over you while you sleep," Hayden said softly, sliding a palm upward until it was over his mate's heart. "From now on, I'm going to do the protecting around here. I'll hold you close all night long, and when you wake in the morning, baby? I'll still be holding you. So, yeah, you just sleep...I'll do the rest."

Chapter Twelve

"Geez, Josh, you're acting like it's a first date or something." Kira kept watching him pace in sympathetic disbelief.

Great. As if it weren't bad enough that he felt iron-winged butterflies in his stomach as he waited for Hayden to show up at his office, now his kid sister was watching him sweat it out.

It's a lunch, he told himself. Only a lunch...date.

"In a way," he told her, drawing in a calming breath, "it is a first date. Well, second date, to be more precise."

"Joshua!" she cried, thunking her forehead with the heel of her palm. "He belongs to you! Didn't you two just spend all of last night together?"

Josh couldn't help it, her blunt comment made him flush a little even if they'd only held each other. Damn, they'd barely kissed at all, just nuzzled and stroked until Josh had drifted into the deepest, most satisfying slumber he'd experienced in years. He'd only woken once, dimly aware that he'd been snoring, his head atop Hayden's chest.

Still, the idea that Kira knew he'd slept in anyone's

bed, any man's—especially one he wanted with downright painful intensity—was just a little too close for comfort. "Don't go there," he growled, stopping to examine his reflection in the mirror that hung on the back of his closed door. "Nothing happened at all. We just slept."

"Yeah, right." Kira chuckled. "I can so see that happening."

He cast an innocent glance at his sister in the mirror, and resumed combing his hair. "That is all."

She giggled. "I guess that's why they call it sleeping together, huh?"

"Kira, we kissed...that's about it."

"Did you share a bed?"

Josh swallowed hard, avoiding her gaze. "All right, we kissed and held each other for a long time," he admitted, hating the way he blushed.

Kira smiled at him in the mirror. "My point, big brother, is that he's your mate. He belongs to you totally." Her tone was playful, yet exasperated when she added, "There's no dating in mating."

He ran quick hands over his curls once more. No matter how short he kept his hair, it always stayed a little unruly. "There's dating leading to mating."

"Yeah, but your sitch is already a done deal. You claimed him five years ago and he claimed you. Having sex again, well, you're just picking things back up."

She sat at the desk behind him, and in the mirror he caught her gaze seriously. "Kira, we never had all that. One date, that was it. If life had been different, we would have had a bunch of dates after joining. Or even before joining. We had nothing. In a way, we've got to get to know each other, okay?"

She smiled at him, staring at him in the reflective glass. "I get it, Joshua. I'm just saying...you don't need to be nervous, sweetie. He loves you. He's all yours. Relax a little."

He grinned slowly, straightening his uniform collar and then smoothing the front of the shirt. "Besides, who says that mates don't keep on dating?" he asked. "You've got to keep the romance alive, right?"

"As if I'd know? I've been in a date drought since, like, high school." She leaned back in his desk chair. "But for the record, Officer Peterson, I don't think keeping the romance hot is going to be an issue for you and Hayden."

A soft knock sounded on the office door and Josh jolted slightly, stepping backward. In a flurry of motion, Kira waved him over to the desk chair, then moved forward to open the door herself. "Come sit down over here. That way you won't look so anxious and overeager." Then with a roll of her eyes and an exaggerated stage whisper added, "For your own mate's arrival."

"You should be more sympathetic," he hissed back, feeling his face flush even hotter.

"You should be more confident!" She smiled and blew him a kiss, then opened the door with a flourish—only to stagger backward in surprise.

Hell yeah, being confronted with a human mountain was one heck of a shock, no doubt. Ben Orson filled the entire doorframe, and at six-foot-seven or so to Kira's diminutive five-foot-three, it was like unexpectedly bumping into a moose. Slowly she craned her head upward until they made eye contact, and Josh smirked. As gentle and beta as his kid sister was, she wasn't easily overwhelmed by anyone—wolf or human, male or female. But quiet, lumbering Ben clearly managed to do it, and by the simple act of appearing in the doorway.

"I'm Ben," he said, his voice a soft rumble. "You're Kira Peterson."

She kept craning her neck to look at him, never even seeing his extended palm. "How'd you know that?"

Kira had only started coming around the station in the past few weeks, and with Ben often out on patrol, they hadn't met. Josh leaned back in his chair, enjoying watching his sister squirm. She deserved to be thrown off her game for once, especially after her earlier teasing.

Ben smiled slowly, that very familiar sideways grin. "Well, I'm an officer of the law, ma'am." He inclined his head politely. "I have my ways of obtaining critical information."

That comment, however, spooked Josh somewhat, reminding him as it did of the eerie way Ben seemed to know about Hayden.

Kira shivered at his remark, almost as if shaking her wolf's coat free of unwelcome water or mud. As if she, too, were unsettled by some unsaid portent in Ben's innocuous words.

Ben glanced down at his still-extended hand, realizing

that Kira couldn't see it, not with her head jacked back so she could look him in the eye. Appearing resolved, he reached down, bending a little, and took hold of Kira's hand. Not in a formal shake, but more of a gentle, curling caress.

"I've known I'd meet you soon," Ben said softly.

Kira shivered again, blinking at Ben as if mesmerized. "Wh-what?"

"You're Josh's sister," he explained with a nod, making it seem that his words hadn't been imbued with mystery and unspoken meaning. "I knew I'd meet you."

"Ohhhh." Kira stared at their joined hands and then quickly squirmed out of Ben's grasp.

Ben smiled down again before lumbering past her and toward Josh. "Uh, Chief has some good news for you, Sarge. He called from the courthouse and asked me to fill you in."

Josh sat up in his desk chair, instantly alert and wondering if this good news related to the Rawlings-Keener case. A vague part of his mind wondered if Hayden would walk in on this meeting, and the thought of Hayden hearing anything at all about those murderous creeps made his blood run cold. Ben kept talking. "Rawlings and Keener? They tried to bring a motion about your undercover work—"

Josh slammed a fist on the desk. "Chief said there was no motion!"

"They tried to bring one to the judge apparently, as of this morning."

"Why wasn't I told?" Josh demanded, his heartbeat racing.

Hayden had to be safe, those thugs had to stay locked up...

"Chief said he hadn't wanted to get you all worked up over nothing."

"That pair filing a motion for dismissal sure as hell isn't nothing."

Kira piped in. "Joshua," she prompted softly, "didn't you hear what Ben said? It's good news, sweetie. Good news."

His pulse calmed a little and he rubbed his brow, instantly covered in sweat. "Go on, Orson," he said after a moment. "I'm listening."

"So, the motion was dismissed as of twenty minutes ago. The trial's been set for next month."

Kira squealed, hurling herself at Josh, both arms looping about his neck. He could only blink at the other officer, stunned, as he folded his kid sister close. Ben smiled at him, a strangely knowing look in his black eyes. "Thought you'd like that."

Ben turned to go, rolling his big shoulders as he moved.

"Hey, Orson!" Josh called after him, and Ben paused, glancing over his shoulder.

"Yeah, Sarge?" One black eyebrow rode upward curiously.

"What did you mean last night? With...you know,

what you said?"

Ben tilted his head slightly as if he had no recollection at all about his hinted promise that Hayden remained alive. "Not sure what you mean there, Peterson."

Josh just shook his head. "I'll get it out of you," he promised with a wry grin. "One way or another, you'll fess up."

Ben was already turning away, but Josh would have sworn—would have laid very big money on the fact—that he heard the giant murmur, "Glad your mate's back."

Lunchtime was always packed at the Over the Moon Saloon, and Hayden was thankful that he'd called ahead. He felt Josh's body press close behind his as they wove their way through the standing-room-only bar crowd. When Hayden had to pause to let a few people pass by, Josh collided into his backside, and for one glorious moment, Hayden reveled in feeling such heat coming off his mate—and right in public.

In fact, when the knot of tourists in front of him surged forward, Hayden stayed put for an extra thirty seconds or so, just to soak in Josh's woodsy, delicious scent. Plus, he loved the fact that his own scent was all over his mate. Yeah, he'd marked the other wolf thoroughly last night. He couldn't help his strong possessive streak. He was Alpha, after all, and he'd finally reclaimed Josh after five long years of separation.

Josh's sturdy hand reached forward, clasping Hayden's forearm. "What's the hold up?" he asked, his view of the aisle blocked by Hayden's larger size and height.

Hayden turned slightly, glancing at Josh. "You," he murmured, giving his lover a demure smile. "I was enjoying the full body contact."

Josh released his arm and gave him a slight shove in the back. "Keep walking, Hay. I'm starved."

Hayden loped forward, his eye on the reserved booth that he'd specifically had set aside for them. As he reached the table, he gave Josh a slightly sheepish glance; Josh released a low, rumbling laugh. It was the same booth they'd sat in seven weeks earlier, that first night they'd met to discuss the elders' mandate.

"Thought we might try this again," Hayden said, sliding into the seat.

Josh stripped off his jacket, fumbled in his pockets for his keys and badge and tossed them onto the table with a meaningful smile. "Gotta be comfortable, you know. For an important talk like this one."

"Here I was thinking it was all about the load in your front pocket," Hayden teased. "You know that's of very keen interest to me."

Josh settled into the booth, reaching for the appetizer menu. He made a big show of reading over it, like he'd never eaten at Over the Moon before in his life. And he blushed. A lot.

"Did I embarrass you?" Hayden asked, swatting Josh with his own menu. Finally the guy looked up and met his gaze. A slight smile began at the edges of his lips, an expression Hayden had once considered a smirk. He knew better now.

Shy. Such a totally shy guy.

"I'm nervous as shit," Josh confessed after a moment, his smile growing broader. "I know, totally lame." He stared down at the table again, avoiding Hayden's intense gaze.

Hayden moved his long legs, pressing them close to Josh's beneath the table. Nobody else could see, but his mate would feel the physical connection, their bodies brushing together. "Your shy streak charms the pants off me, baby," he said. "But you don't have any reason to be nervous with me. Never."

Hayden moved his legs again, pinning Josh's own knees between his own. Holding him tight until Josh slowly lifted his gaze. As always, his unusual, beautiful eyes stole Hayden's breath. "God, you gorgeous thing, you. I'm glad you waited for me."

Josh laughed, raking a hand over his short hair. "Like I'd have given up."

"You might've."

His mate shook his head. "Not on you, Hay. Not a chance." Then Josh leaned back in the booth, much more relaxed. "So, what do you plan to do about the elders' mandate? We missed their deadline."

Hayden's heart skipped a beat. "But...we're...What do you mean? I didn't think that mattered."

Joshua's face split into a huge, wonderful smile. "Gotcha."

"You little fucker. For a minute I actually thought..."

"You deserve a little payback for all the worrying you put me through," Josh said, taking a sip of water. "But today's too important. Too special for me to give you shit."

Hayden nodded in agreement. "Big stuff. The rest of our lives, and all that."

Josh planted both elbows on the table, leaning in toward Hayden. "Actually," he said in a quiet, sultry voice, "I was thinking more like our first date. I've got to make a very good impression."

"Second date," Hayden corrected, eyes lowering so that his lashes dropped seductively. "We did the first date thing five years ago."

Josh slid one palm across the table slowly, daring to graze fingertips against Hayden's knuckles. "You didn't lose respect for me just 'cause I gave it all up on the first night out, did you?"

Hayden turned his palm, threading his fingers together with Josh's. "No, but I'm willing to start over at first base. And lucky us, there is no second base so we can go straight to third."

When the bartender approached, they released their hold on each other, snapping apart guiltily. Thank God it was a man they both knew, Jake Orson, whose brother Ben worked with Josh. Jake had been on their baseball team back in high school so the three of them went back a long way, and like just about everyone else in their relatively small town, Jake knew Hayden was gay.

As for Josh and his sexual orientation, however, it

would be a definite Jackson newsflash, and Hayden would leave that up to his mate. Josh's timetable, his choice, just as it had been for Hayden. Besides, it was going to be even trickier for Josh as an officer of the law, so Hayden knew that the process might take a little time. Not that he cared. He had Josh back in his life, in his arms and heart—and his bed. Everything else was just window dressing to him.

Jake sauntered up to the table with a lazy grin on his face, acting as if he'd never seen the handholding—or the fast "drop and part" cover up job they'd done. Jake plonked down two beer coasters and a set of full menus. "Hello, boys. Big lunch today?" Jake's eyes held Hayden's for a moment, an oddly knowing gleam in those clear blue depths. So much for attributing the gift of subtlety to their bartender friend.

Shit. Hayden hadn't really considered that calling ahead for reservations might look like a date, and thereby out Josh.

"It's a celebration, actually," Josh explained smoothly. "Jake, it's a very big day."

Hayden stared at his mate and did his level best to keep his chin from dropping. What exactly was Josh about to reveal to their old high school acquaintance?

Josh leaned back in the booth with a big, satisfied grin plastered on his face, and continued, "Yeah, I spent the past five years pursuing this pair of thugs, and just found out they're going to trial next month."

Hayden's eyes grew wide and disbelieving as he stared

at the other wolf; he felt his throat go dry. "Is...is it?" he sputtered.

Josh leaned forward then, and boldly took Hayden's hand in his own, drawing it to his lips. With a brushing kiss he replied, "Yeah, baby, hadn't had the chance to tell you yet."

For one long, endless moment they simply stared at each other, and then still holding Hayden's hand, Josh looked up at Jake Orson. To Jake's credit, the bartender never so much as blinked at the public display of very gay affection. Josh smiled up at him. "Your brother's the one who gave me the great news."

"Ben? He's actually good for something down at the station? I figured he just slept and ate all the time like he does at home." Jake laughed at his own joke.

"He's been remarkably helpful lately."

"Yeah, my brother's good that way." Jake nodded and gave Josh a serious look. "He's always got your back. Don't forget that."

Hayden would have sworn that some mystical understanding passed between his lover and Jake Orson right then, some kind of private message, but before he could wonder what it meant, Jake had bounded away, leaving them alone.

Hayden began playing with his coaster, staring down at the table. "I can't believe you kissed my hand in front of him," he admitted quietly, not looking up.

Josh leaned forward and this time he took hold of both Hayden's hands, squeezing them for emphasis. "The whole town's gonna know we're together by week's end anyway. You know what Jackson's like. I spent the night at your place last night; you'll be at mine later on tonight. Now we've been seen at lunch together. Hell, the news about us being a couple will spread faster than I can bother blushing over the fact."

"Will I?" Hayden asked, daring to lift his gaze. Josh studied him, not understanding, so Hayden clarified. "Will I spend the night at your place tonight?"

Joshua didn't answer at first, obviously giving the question serious consideration. After a moment, he leaned much closer. "It's like this, Garrett. We're gonna date a while, right? Because I want to know everything about you and because I want to woo you. Just like I promised I would a couple of months ago. We were robbed of that, and I'm gonna give you every damned thing that was stolen from you."

Hayden swallowed hard, deeply moved. "I...I want that, Joshua. I'd love that."

"But just so you know, Hayden—just so we are totally clear—you are already mine. That means every night we sleep in each other's arms. Every morning we wake still tangled together. I can't spend one night without you, without feeling your body and knowing your scent's on me, even if I am courting you."

"Courting me, huh?" Hayden really did blush then as his mate's sensual, claiming words sank in. "I never knew how old fashioned you could be."

"Much as I love you, much as you love me—we've got

a lot to learn about each other," Josh said gently, and for a moment—with his hair rumpled from his wool cap, and the flush high in his cheeks—he looked a lot like he had on that long ago day out on the tarmac. Hayden felt a rush of love for the man that was almost more intense than any he'd ever known. It was so strong, his eyes watered at the intensity of it and he had to glance away. They'd been so young, so innocent, and Josh was right—they'd been robbed of far too much.

And then he recalled the night they'd first made love, how surprisingly shy Joshua had turned out to be, so inexperienced at being with another man. Hayden had only begun to show him how it would be between them physically before everything was stolen from them. Before Josh had been brutally violated—after Hayden had been so careful and gentle with him. God, he'd wanted to spare Josh any pain during their lovemaking, and then...

He shook his head, clearing the dark memories. They would start over now, as if it was the very first time all over again, as if none of the nightmarishly bad shit had ever happened. For some reason, that thought didn't sadden him now as it might It awakened him.

"Yeah, we've got a whole lot to learn. And I've got a lot to teach you," Hayden whispered, meeting his mate's gaze with suggestive, highly sexual intensity. His heart slammed hard inside his chest, and his pulse skittered in arousal as he imagined long, slow moments of instruction while holding Josh in his arms. "I'd only begun tutoring you that night five years ago."

Hayden caught a strong aroma right then, wafting

from the other side of the booth: Joshua's very distinctive mating scent. Josh glanced at his watch, then back at Hayden. He released a rumbling growl of possession. "Maybe I could manage an afternoon off just this once. You know, for the sake of, uh, higher learning."

Hayden smiled, sniffing at the air, loving that his mate was marking him all over again, right here in the bar. "Of course every teacher must also be willing to be a student himself," he said with a husky promise all his own. "And keep up with the latest field research, of course."

Josh slipped a leg up against Hayden's right then, rubbing it back and forth sensually, as if he were in wolf form and hoping to be petted. Hayden flashed on an image of his mate transformed, that glorious, gleaming coat shining beneath the full moon as they ran together. Breathless, inspired. In love.

Swallowing hard, he tamped down the overwhelming urge to howl his emotions to the entire saloon. Instead, he leaned forward and whispered, "Full moon in two nights, mate. I have plans for you." With that husky, arousing promise, Hayden intentionally released a potent mating scent, but it wasn't like he could've prevented himself from doing so anyway. Not with Josh sitting across from him, all gorgeous and flush-faced, that sexed-up expression in his light eyes.

No, Hayden couldn't have kept his mating and arousal scents corked if he'd tried. He was hopelessly aroused, and any other wolf in the bar would know it now because those scents were flowing off his skin like rich cologne. And Josh clearly got the message—because he jerked his head back, pegging Hayden with a wild stare. His hands tensed against the tabletop, and his eyes changed to a much darker hue. They stared at each other, breathing heavily from arousal and then Josh slowly tilted his chin upward, sniffing at the air without ever taking his gaze off Hayden. After several moments, Josh's eyes slid shut and he swallowed hard.

"You'd better get me out of here, Garrett. Fast. At least if you're going to keep that up."

"I love it when you call me Garrett," Hayden purred back, laughing low. "It's hot as hell, baby."

Josh's hands clenched against the edge of the table and his jaw began ticking. "I should have claimed you last night. Not waited...why did we choose to wait?" he asked, shaking his head and swallowing several times. "That mating scent you're putting off is about to make me do dangerous things—right here, right now. In public. You've gotta stop, Hayden. Please."

"You don't like my mating scent?" Hayden asked languidly.

Josh's eyes slowly drifted open. "That," he said in a husky, deep voice, "is most definitely not the problem."

Hayden leaned forward and slowly stroked the back of Josh's hand. "Well, Officer Peterson, I suggest you call the chief and request the afternoon off, like you said. Because my tutoring? All that I want to teach you? It's already begun. That's what you're scenting right now."

Josh pegged him with an almost hopeless expression,

there was that much desire awash in his gaze—as if the simple act of getting the check and leaving the bar was more than he could bear. Hayden grinned, recalling that long ago night when they'd pounced on each other in the front seat of Josh's truck, unable to even make the drive home in their desperation to touch each other.

Quickly deciding to make things easier for his mate, Hayden gave a gallant half bow and rose to his feet. "Let's forget about lunch," he said quietly. "You make that call."

Chapter Thirteen

"This feels familiar," Hayden said softly, turning to face Josh in the front seat of his mate's Tahoe. "The two of us together, here in the front seat of your truck. Me dying to make love to you. You looking flushed and gorgeous."

Josh lifted an eyebrow. "We're both wearing clothes this time."

"And you're not climbing on top of me, ready to go to town. Of course, that could be arranged," Hayden added in a sultry voice, patting his lap in invitation. "My wolf want to come over and be petted?"

Josh said nothing, just grinned, running his hands along the steering wheel in a sweeping motion. Totally shy, all over again, Hayden thought. And totally charming because of it.

"You're nervous again," Hayden observed.

"A little bit," Josh confessed, staring at the house and still sliding both palms along the steering wheel in a back-and-forth motion. "I mean, it's like it was that night, the first time. I want you so bad it's killing me, Hayden, but it's getting down to it that's kind of hard to tangle my way through."

Hayden lifted a hand to his mate's cheek, stroking it slowly with his knuckles. "You don't need to be anxious. Not with me."

Josh seemed to catch his edgy gesture with the steering wheel. Stopping himself, he let his hands fall loose against his thighs. Josh cut his eyes sideways. "I still am, though, and not just because I've spent so long aching for you. I mean, five years is an eternity, but it's more than how long it's been." Josh blew out a sigh, staring straight ahead at his house—at the door that their attackers had broken down.

Hayden reached for his mate's hand, and drew it against his own thigh. "Baby, we don't have to make love yet. We can go as slow as you need. I know what happened to you."

Josh's eyes slid shut, his jaw tensing visibly. "I hate that you know. I despise that you...that you think of that dirty, horrid shit when you even consider touching me."

Hayden grabbed Josh's arm, forcing the wolf to turn in his seat. "Joshua," he commanded firmly, but Josh kept staring away. "Joshua, look at me. Now."

With a staggered inhalation, Josh slowly turned his gaze on Hayden. Tears shone in his eyes and he swallowed hard. Such vulnerability was a striking contrast to his crisp police uniform, an outward image of his strong Alpha strength. "I hate that you know I was touched by anyone other than you," he admitted, "but especially that you know it was them."

"Them?" Hayden blinked. "It was both?"

Josh flinched and then nodded. "I guess...yeah, you were unconscious. How could you have known?"

"I remember all that they threatened," Hayden said tightly. "I just didn't know it was both of them."

"It doesn't matter," Josh said dully. "What does matter, though, Hayden, is you associating that with me. With loving me...with touching me."

"My feelings for you have absolutely nothing to do with those men. Don't you understand that I have to be gentle with you? I would be no matter what. Which has got absolutely nothing to do with what happened to you. It's about how much I love you. How I want to make you feel when we're together like that."

Josh scowled, a disgusted look coming over his features. "But why else would you keep talking about...well, being so careful with me?" Josh asked quietly, still staring up at the door to his house.

Hayden reached for Josh's hand, taking it into his own. "Because you only ever had me one time, and that was a long while ago. It hurt you enough then. Of course I'm going to take my time with you, going to make it sweet for you, baby. So sweet."

Josh nodded, staring into his lap. "Okay, I'll admit it straight up. I am totally terrified." He burst out laughing, meeting Hayden's gaze. "It's like...like I'm twenty-two all over again, and you're gonna get me drunk, but this time I already know you're going to make me see fucking constellations and exploding stars just by touching me. I already know you're going to start slow, and then work me into an absolute frenzy. It's all the same awkward terror, you see, but this time I realize exactly how it's going to be. Which just makes it even more...overwhelming."

Hayden slid as close to Josh as he could and pulled him into a tender embrace. Josh folded into it, burying his face in the crook of Hayden's neck. Hayden felt the warmth of his mate's breath, the slight scraping of his beard growth. Suddenly he missed that soft tickling goatee that Josh had worn five years earlier. "Would you grow your beard again for me?" he murmured against the top of Josh's head. "I loved the goatee."

"I'll give you anything you want, Garrett. Anything. You know that."

Hayden stroked his fingertips across Josh's cheek and whispered, "Then trust me. Trust me and don't be afraid. But are you really ready for this step? To become lovers again?"

Josh pulled back so that he could stare up into Hayden's eyes. "I want you, Alpha. I've spent five years waiting for this moment. So, yes, I'm willing and ready."

Hayden suddenly remembered Josh's promise that night at the bar two months earlier. He couldn't help flushing in anticipation as he recalled that pledge.

"Eager and gentle, too?" he asked, loosening Josh's belt. As he did so, the man's fly jutted out from the erection that obviously thickened at the promise of being touched. "That's what you offered me, as I recall."

Josh gave him a sideways smile. The very same one

Hayden had once wrongly assumed was cocky and smug. "Well, you were very gentle with me when we got together...and extremely eager. Least I could do was grant the same in return."

"Actually," Hayden said, pulling Josh's shirt loose from inside his pants and unfastening the last button so that the uniform fell open, "I think I'd prefer you flushed and desperate like you got with me as the night went on."

Josh brushed at his hair, glancing away. "I couldn't stop myself, Hayden. You're too damn hot and gorgeous." Slowly he slid his gaze back to Hayden's face, lowering his lashes. "In fact, I'm not convinced of how gentle either of us is going to be in a few minutes."

Hayden tilted his head sideways. "Kiss me, cowboy. Kiss me and take me any way you want me. I love you. That's all that matters...we'll figure out the rest along the way."

Josh pressed his lips against Hayden's then, just the softest brush of their mouths together. In that hesitant, tender stroke, Hayden felt the earth begin to quake. Knew that their years of pent-up longing were about to come pouring out. Very softly, Josh kissed him, murmuring, "I think this time we should have white wine."

Josh opened his fridge, desperately hoping that Kira hadn't helped herself to the bottle of Chardonnay he'd bought at Albertson's the other day. If she had, he was going to skin the fur off her little body when she got home. He bent down so he could look for the bottle, and wanted to shout in relief when he spotted it in the lower section of the door. As he reached down for it, Hayden's left arm came around him from behind. "Here," his mate said, taking the bottle of wine, "allow me."

Then Hayden moved right up behind him, sliding his other arm about Josh's belly. Josh stood perfectly still as Hayden splayed his palm across Josh's uniform-clad waist. His belt remained unfastened, his fly was now unsnapped, and for one tempting moment Hayden worked at his zipper, lowering it partway.

"Not yet," Hayden whispered, leaving Josh's pants half-open, and moved to kiss his nape. Hayden's mouth lingered there against the tender flesh, and he trailed hot kisses up into Josh's curling hair and then nuzzled him. "Sorry," Hayden murmured with a satisfied sigh. "Just couldn't help myself. Seeing you lean over into the fridge, uh...it was a stunning visual, to say the least."

Josh laughed low. "Well, who said I wasn't trying to give you ideas, huh, Garrett?"

"A totally hard-body cop showing me his ass—while leaning over with his legs slightly spread— would give even a straight man ideas, baby. But since you're my totally built, ripped cop, I'd have to knock those ideas right out of straight boy's head if he ever tried to act on them."

Josh laughed even harder, slowly turning in Hayden's embrace. As Josh looked up his lover's eyes, so intensely blue they were like the color of a Wyoming winter sky, he blurted, "I love you so damned much."

And, God, but it was true. He loved Hayden Garrett so deeply that at times he couldn't breathe from the emotion. Hayden's response was to tilt his head sideways and capture Josh's mouth, much harder than he had at any other time in the past day. With teeth and tongue and a soft groan, Hayden kissed him roughly, his free hand working at Josh's nape, stroking his curls. Then just as swiftly, Hayden broke the kiss, stepping backward. He held up the unopened bottle of wine. "Let's get this stuff flowing."

"I was liking the kiss," Josh offered, walking toward the utensil drawer.

"Yeah, you were," Hayden agreed softly. "But you were shaking all over, too. I want to take that edge off for you, baby. I want to make you see those constellations and stars."

Josh flushed at hearing his earlier confession repeated, and realized that, indeed, he was shaking all over. "It's not fear," he admitted, staring at the linoleum floor. Slowly he looked up, finding Hayden's beautiful eyes wide and fixed on him. "It's need."

His mate nodded, then returned to opening the bottle of wine. "You're not afraid at all?" Hayden asked quietly. "Of me or...being touched by me?"

Josh closed the fridge and leaned back against it, resolved. There was something he had to get Hayden to understand, make him realize—at least if they had any future together as lovers. He drew in a deep breath and forced himself to look at his mate as he spoke. "Hayden, listen," he said quietly, his bone-deep shaking

204

intensifying. "You need to know something. I won't be reliving what they did to me when you and I make love. You've got to understand, that's not how it's gonna be. It was you I gave my virginity to on that night, not them."

Hayden nodded, twisting the cork on the bottle, then paused. "Maybe we should switch things around this time," he said. "I mean, to begin with, not like last time."

Josh shook his head. "That's not what I want," he said, determined to press ahead. He had to say it all or Hayden might always worry about the rape, let it get between them. Josh drew in a strong breath and said, "I spent five years remembering the feel of your hands on me, not reliving how Keener and Rawlings violated me. You are what I've memorized. Your body, your love, your touch...the hardness of you in me, around me, on top of me," he confessed in a heated rush. "And in a few minutes? When you take me under you and make love to me again—finally—I'm going to be giving you myself all over again. Not thinking about those bastards who tried to take you from me."

Hayden turned then, arms spread wide and just stood that way, eyes filled with tears. "I'll tell you what I said a long time ago, Joshua. Do you remember?"

Josh smiled a little. "You said a lot of things."

Hayden walked toward him, arms still open. "I'm going to make this sweet for you, baby. It won't be like any woman you've ever had."

Josh's smile grew much wider as Hayden captured him in a strong embrace. "No kidding, you sexy moron,"

Josh murmured against his lover's chest. "It's gonna be you."

Josh led Hayden down the hallway, past both his room and Kira's, until they reached the living room. Well, he made one quick stop—in the bathroom, grabbing a small tube that he'd had in the drawer for longer than he cared to admit, always hoping for this moment. After grabbing that lube, he kept moving, practically dragging Hayden by the hand toward the end of the hall.

Something told him it was a pretty good idea to steer clear of his own bedroom, even though he'd switched rooms with Kira when she'd moved in. Still, the bed was the same, and with his mate already worrying about him, a fresh start was in order.

Hayden walked into the living room, his gaze moving from the fireplace to the roomy leather sofa. "Seems you have a plan in mind," he said, folding arms across his chest. The gesture did nothing to hide the significant bulge that formed in the front of the man's jeans, either— especially when he rocked back on his heels. "Very cozy setup you got here, Joshua."

"I kinda thought you'd like this room," Josh admitted, moving to turn on the gas logs. Outside the large uncovered windows, there was a beautiful view of firs and lazily falling snow, and inside, with the fire roaring to life, was the perfect location for making love all afternoon long.

"I'm not looking at the room." Hayden's gaze was laser-locked right on Josh, his blue eyes dark with desire.

Josh slowly turned, putting his back to the fire. "So what we gonna do, Garrett? Count off and jump each other?" Josh felt a kick of nervous adrenaline at just making the suggestion.

His mate answered by slowly moving toward the sofa. "Come sit down, Joshua, and I'll show you what I have in mind."

Josh felt his feet moving almost of their own volition and he complied, sitting down on the leather couch. As soon as he did, Hayden knelt down right in front of him, sliding both large palms onto his thighs. Their gazes locked for a breathless, expectant moment.

Yeah, Josh knew exactly what Hayden intended, wanted.

"It'll take the edge off for real," Hayden advised, eyes growing even darker with lust and need. Very slowly he pressed against Josh's thighs, opening them wider. Much wider. And he leaned into the V with his whole body, dragging Josh's mouth down for a staggering kiss while working at Josh's fly with his free hand.

In response, Josh's erection strained even harder in the tight confines of his pants, and he reached down, eager to help Hayden with the job. But his lover halted the motion, stilling Josh's hand with his own. "That's my job," Hayden murmured, barely breaking their kiss and Josh felt the zipper tug downward, cool air meeting his already heated skin.

Leaning back into the sofa, Josh let his eyes slide closed, felt his mate tugging the pants low until his cock sprang free. With a groan, he relished the rough warmth of Hayden's hand closing about his length—and was shocked when that sensation was replaced by warm wetness. His eyes popped open and he looked down to find Hayden's head lowered, an utterly gorgeous expression on his face as he drew Josh's thick length deep into his mouth.

"Oh, God," Josh whispered. Somehow he'd not expected this intimacy. Maybe because they'd bypassed it the first time, or maybe because they'd spent so much time talking about making love. His hips rose up off the sofa, his whole body reacting with a hot shiver of pleasure. Hayden gave Josh's pants a stern yank, and they fell, pooling low about his ankles. Then, rising up slightly, Hayden re-angled his whole body and Josh surged much deeper into his mouth, right as his lover began a strong suctioning and swirling sensation that just about had Josh losing it already.

He moaned, riding up off the couch once again, and sank fingertips into Hayden's hair. Barely, he managed to bark, "Slower! Garrett...slow down." Shit, he wanted to experience this in real time, not rocket launch into Hayden's mouth before they'd even gotten going.

Hayden slowly slid his tongue to the very tip, swirling it in an erotic, tantalizing sweep that caused Josh to grip the wolf's shoulders with both hands. He dug fingers into the fleece that covered such hard, delicious flesh just beneath. Why hadn't he ordered Hayden around a little bit, too? Why hadn't he forced his mate out of his clothes before they got started?

"I need you...naked." Josh tried tugging on the fleece, but as before, Hayden stilled his hand.

With a breathless gasp, Hayden slid Josh's erection from within his mouth, still holding the hard cock firmly in hand. "I'm taking care of you right now," Hayden explained, dragging in a breath. "In every way, Joshua. Just let me love you."

Their eyes met for a moment and Josh finally whispered. "Could you at least take that fleece off? I need to feel your skin against me."

Hayden nodded and with a fast, ripping gesture, was suddenly bare-chested right between Josh's thighs. The eyeful would have been enough to send Josh to the edge as it was, but the view of those rippling, gorgeous shoulder muscles and biceps, combined with the slick warmth of being dragged into the man's mouth again, well, he felt his balls draw tight and high in automatic reaction.

His hands began roaming all across Hayden's smooth shoulders and back, his hips thrusting up and down, all of it as if his body were in control—not his own will. In response, Hayden gripped his hips tightly in both palms, working Josh's rhythmic motion, controlling it, speeding it even as Hayden's mouth quickened across the hard flesh. With a fevered cry, Josh surged upward and felt a quaking spasm of release. Hayden took hold of Josh's buttocks right then, drawing him higher and deeper and holding him fast. Riding out the waves, drinking Josh dry until with one final surging moan, Josh's hips sank down. His cock grew soft and Hayden released it with a sweet kiss, lapping at the tip with his tongue. Josh collapsed, his buttocks resting in Hayden's open grasp against the sofa.

Josh sucked at air, tried to breathe at all, lolling his head against the couch cushions. There between his legs, Hayden made a low growling sound of pleasure and buried his forehead against Josh's abdomen, softly rubbing it back and forth. "You're so beautiful," Hayden murmured, then he finally rested his cheek against Josh's muscular thigh.

Hayden stared up at him, and the only thing Josh could think as he looked back was the very thing he blurted. "You look absolutely fuckable right now. The look on your face...never seen anything like it."

Hayden nuzzled Josh's belly as if they were in wolf form, playing and tumbling. Josh's cock began to fill out again, growing slightly rigid.

Hayden stared up at him in surprise. "Ready again so soon?"

Josh smiled at him, stroking his fingers through Hayden's long dark hair. "I can be ready sooner than you think."

"But it's me doing the worshipping right now, remember?" Hayden slid his hands free, capturing Josh around the waist as he rose up on his knees. "And I've got you relaxed just like I want you. If you're ready for me, that is."

At that promise, Josh felt a further stirring in his groin, a kick that said he was definitely ready, as his cock became infused with blood and heat, growing rigid again.

Hayden moved atop Josh, urging him down onto his back. It was a good thing that the couch was so deep and big, he thought, as they stretched out on it. After some juggling—a misplaced knee, a tangled arm, a knotted T-shirt, some awkward giggling—they were locked tight. Hayden atop Josh, positioned right between his parted thighs, both their bodies smooth and hot and naked.

And primed. Totally and perfectly primed for what was about to happen next.

For a long moment, Hayden just stared down into those exotic, luminous eyes that had first beguiled him years before. The golden-green seemed to be darker than usual, flecked with more amber. In the hush, they just gazed at each other, wrestling for each breath. Aware of bare skin against bare skin, of hard hips pushing together.

Poised. Knowing that in a moment, union would begin, that first push of Hayden as he entered Josh. They were both slicked up, totally ready, but somehow this one moment was the breath-stealer. This heartbeat of just staring into each other's eyes without uttering one word or sound.

Josh reached up, brushing fingertips through Hayden's long hair that had fallen across his cheek. Eyes still locked on Hayden, he drew the lock to his nose and sniffed, giving him a meaningful look. Yes, you are still my mate, that gaze said. Now, more than ever before. And we are about to deepen that bond.

Then Josh slowly drew the lock of hair to his lips and kissed the ends. Right as the heady, seductive aroma of his mating scent began to weave about Hayden.

"You're marking me," Hayden finally whispered, filled with as much wonder right now as he'd been all those years before. "You're covering me in your scent."

His mate smiled up at him, lifted his calves higher and murmured, "Claim me back, Garrett. Take me all the way home."

Hayden pressed hard right then, gave his hips enough force to fulfill Josh's request, but did so with caution. It was critical that he hold himself back, at least enough to keep the moment as painless as possible. "Don't," Josh groaned hoarsely in his ear. "Don't...go slow. Now. All of you. Now."

"Joshua," Hayden murmured, sliding his palms up under the man's lower back, arching him for a better angle. But he made sure to continue progressing slowly, only penetrating Josh one inch at a time.

Josh grunted, tangling both arms about Hayden's neck and locked his legs about Hayden's torso. "Damn it, Garrett! I need you!" he cried out, seizing hold of Hayden with his entire body.

Hayden cursed low, and decided to give his mate all of himself. Fast, hard, no hesitation. With more force than he thought wise, he surged inside Josh, who barked out sharp curses, wincing and moaning all at the same time.

Hayden stilled, suspended in time, holding his breath.

He was all the way in, and Josh was tense as iron beneath him, his expression frozen in that mask of pain. Until the pain faded, Josh's features relaxing, the harsh lines about his mouth vanishing. Until very slowly his mouth turned upward, forming a smile.

And his eyes flew open, filled with the deepest, most satisfied look that Hayden had ever seen on any man's face. "You hit the sweet spot," he said in a husky purr. "Now keep on going, baby. You are all the way home."

With that declaration, Josh began marking him thoroughly, from the crown of his head to the tips of his toes. That primal, claiming aroma was so intense that Hayden knew that every wolf in Jackson would know the truth the moment they met him. That Hayden Garrett had already been claimed.

He belonged fully and completely to Joshua Peterson. For life.

There were at least sixty wolves gathered in the midnight clearing, some larger, some smaller—male, female, old, young. But the main thing that struck Josh as he stared across their gathered kind was that members from both their packs mingled. Peacefully.

Hayden paused beside him, pawing at the ground as he surveyed the wolves from behind the trees. They stood together, shoulder to shoulder, radiating their mating warmth. With a light yelp, Joshua pounced at Hayden, tumbling him to the forest floor. For a moment, they rolled together, growling and nuzzling. This union, the one they experienced as wolf-mates, was one of Josh's favorite moments with Hayden. It was innocent, playful...infused

213

with freedom.

After a moment, a familiar wolf appeared a few feet away, interrupting their playful tussling. Kira. She tilted her head sideways, her gentle impatience obvious, even when she was in wolf form.

It was time to greet the packs, to join the mating celebration. This full moon was the most important one their two packs had known in decades: unity had come. All because he, Joshua Peterson, had fallen in love with another Alpha. Because he'd taken the lovely, mysterious wolf beside him as lifemate.

Hayden clearly knew his thoughts, trotting to his side. They fell in step, walking proudly and together into the circle of fellow wolves. Josh lifted his head high, put his ears back and released a song toward the sky.

Right then, the huge pregnant moon appeared from behind parted clouds, bathing all of them in magnificent silver.

Joshua howled his pleasure at the beautiful image, loving the way Hayden's coat was painted in mysterious light. Stunning. Beautiful.

Josh released another wolf's cry, a long, heartfelt one. He is mine, Josh sang to the moon. My wolf mate is mine...and he is home. We are home together. And we are free.

About the Author

Cooper Davis is a lifelong writer and reader who fell in love with books as a child thanks to a cadre of powerful women: Trixie Belden, Nancy Drew and Betsy, Tacy and Tibb. But it was Scarlet O'Hara who truly kicked her into gear, inspiring Cooper's first short story. Scarlet may have launched Cooper's writerly game of casting herself as the heroine (what woman wouldn't want to wear that red dress, even if it marked her a harlot?), but that passion continued long past the discovery of Jane Austen. Cooper writes paranormal and is an avid reader of many genres.

To learn more about Cooper Davis, please visit www.CooperDavisBooks.com. Send an e-mail to Cooper at Cooper@CooperDavisBooks.com.

GREAT CHEAP FUN

Discover eBooks!

THE FASTEST WAY TO GET THE HOTTEST NAMES

Get your favorite authors on your favorite reader, long before they're out in print! Ebooks from Samhain go wherever you go, and work with whatever you carry—Palm, PDF, Mobi, Kindle, nook, and more.

SAMHAIN
PUBLISHING

WWW.SAMHAINPUBLISHING.COM